SPECIAL MESSAGE TO READERS

THE ULVERSCROFT FOUNDATION
(registered UK charity number 264873)

was established in 1972 to provide funds for research, diagnosis and treatment of eye diseases. Examples of major projects funded by the Ulverscroft Foundation are:-

- The Children's Eye Unit at Moorfields Eye Hospital, London
- The Ulverscroft Children's Eye Unit at Great Ormond Street Hospital for Sick Children
- Funding research into eye diseases and treatment at the Department of Ophthalmology, University of Leicester
- The Ulverscroft Vision Research Group, Institute of Child Health
- Twin operating theatres at the Western Ophthalmic Hospital, London
- The Chair of Ophthalmology at the Royal Australian College of Ophthalmologists

You can help further the work of the Foundation by making a donation or leaving a legacy. Every contribution is gratefully received. If you would like to help support the Foundation or require further information, please contact:

THE ULVERSCROFT FOUNDATION
The Green, Bradgate Road, Anstey
Leicester LE7 7FU, England
Tel: (0116) 236 4325
website: www.foundation.ulverscroft.com

GIVE THE GIRL A GUN

Manville Moon is a private investigator. On a night out with his girlfriend Fausta Moreni, the lovely owner of the El Patio Café, a group of customers invites them both to a private party at an inventor's home, to celebrate the launch of a business venture based on his new device. But soon after their arrival, the inventor is shot dead by an unseen assailant. Police suspicion quickly falls on the boyfriend of one of the guests, and Moon is hired to prove his innocence — plunging him and Fausta into deadly danger . . .

Books by Richard Deming
in the Linford Mystery Library:

THE GALLOWS IN MY GARDEN
TWEAK THE DEVIL'S NOSE

RICHARD DEMING

GIVE THE GIRL A GUN

Complete and Unabridged

LINFORD
Leicester

First published in Great Britain

First Linford Edition
published 2016

Copyright © 1954 by Richard Deming
All rights reserved

*A catalogue record for this book is available
from the British Library.*

ISBN 978–1–4448–2986–0

Published by
F. A. Thorpe (Publishing)
Anstey, Leicestershire

Set by Words & Graphics Ltd.
Anstey, Leicestershire
Printed and bound in Great Britain by
T. J. International Ltd., Padstow, Cornwall

This book is printed on acid-free paper

1

By now I should be used to the attention Fausta Moreni draws in public, for I have squired her across enough night club floors amid the drooling of every male customer and the homicidal glares of every female. Yet as always when her passage turned every head, none of which so much as flicked a glance at me, I had to suppress an impulse to cross my eyes, put both thumbs in my ears and wiggle the fingers just to test my theory that she made me invisible.

Fausta's own club, El Patio, was the scene of this gauntlet-running, and we were on our way out. On the infrequent occasions we spent an evening together, they always started like that, for the stairs from Fausta's apartment on the second floor of El Patio lead to a hall at the rear of the club, and in order to get out of the place you have to traverse the whole length of the dining room and one end of the cocktail lounge.

Fausta, also as always, dragged out our exit an unreasonable length of time by playing the hostess clear across the dining room. At every table we passed, she smiled at the customers and dropped a gracious 'Good evening.' When she knew a customer by name, which involved about every third table, she stopped for a moment's chat.

To my past bitter objection that when she took a night off, she ought to take it off completely, she always explained that devoting a few seconds of personal attention to her customers bred goodwill. But why a supper club which nightly turned away people without reservations required further goodwill, she has never explained to my satisfaction.

We were almost to the door when a young fellow at a table for six hailed her. He was a handsome lad in an underdeveloped sort of way: thin, curly-haired, white-toothed and actually possessing dimples. There were three couples at the table and apparently his date was the slim, fresh-looking redhead on his left.

'Fausta!' he called. 'Come drink a toast to our future.'

Fausta flashed him a friendly smile and said, 'Thank you, Barney, but we are just leaving.'

'Not without wishing us luck,' Barney insisted.

He stood up and gestured with a half-full champagne bottle.

'Oh!' Fausta said in a delighted voice. 'You and Madeline are getting married?'

For an instant the young man looked blank. Then he flushed slightly. Across the table a heavy-set middle-aged man who looked vaguely familiar, but whom I could not quite place, erupted into a roar of laughter. The redhead on Barney's left blushed furiously.

'Now you'll have to ask her, Barney,' the heavy-set man said in a rubbery voice. 'You compromised her publicly.'

Fausta gave the redhead a contrite look. 'I have made a *faux pas*, Madeline? I am sorry.'

The redhead continued to blush and Barney laughed a trifle uncertainly. 'That would call for an even bigger celebration,' he said. 'But unfortunately Madeline's planning to marry another guy one of these days, and only regards me as a business associate. Tonight we're just celebrating the incorporation of the Huntsafe Company.'

When Fausta merely looked politely puzzled, the red-haired Madeline said, 'Barney got word today that the patent application on the Gimmick was approved.' She had a clear, pleasant voice which somehow fitted her fresh appearance.

'Oh? You mean that thing with which you shoot deer?'

Barney grinned at her. 'You weren't listening when I explained it, Fausta. It's not to shoot deer, it's to avoid shooting deer hunters. But sit down at least long enough to have a drink.'

Fausta glanced inquiringly over her shoulder at me. I shrugged, having learned not to waste effort trying to influence her minor decisions, as she invariably does as she pleases anyway. This time she apparently decided she should make amends for her *faux pas* by accepting the invitation.

Signaling a nearby waiter for a couple of extra chairs, she took my hand, drew me up beside her and said, 'I would like you people to meet Manville Moon.'

The curly-haired young man she introduced as Bernard Amhurst, and the redhead as Madeline Strong. When she designated the heavy-set man who had guffawed as being Edgar Friday, I understood why he had seemed familiar.

Ed Friday was supposed to be an ex-racketeer, though certain people with a thorough knowledge of what went on in town seemed a trifle dubious about the 'ex.' Open local gossip said he had accumulated his pile in the extortion racket years back, but just prior to World War II had dissolved his underworld connections and invested his ill-gotten gains in legitimate business, primarily in a couple of wartime manufacturing plants and in a chain of grocery stores. Less overt gossip whispered that the switch from extortion to respectable money-making operations did not represent complete reform, and in addition to legitimate enterprise he had dabbled in wartime black market, shady steel speculation, and had cut a big slice of profit from the war-surplus-material racket.

Whatever the truth, he was clean insofar as his official record was concerned. During his extortion days he had been lucky enough never to have gotten tagged, and now that he was supposed to have graduated to the more refined but more lucrative schemes, where purchased influence and sharp dealing were the weapons instead of guns and clubs, he was beyond the range of a municipal rackets squad. If the whispers were true, it would take either a Congressional investigation or the Federal tax boys to upset his applecart.

The woman with Friday, a sleek brunette of about thirty who gave the impression she had been bathed, dressed, made up and then lacquered so that her total effect was permanently fixed and would remain flawless even in a wind storm, was named Evelyn Karnes and was in 'show business.' Whether as a Metropolitan Opera star or as a strip-teaser, no one made clear. On her wrist I noted a bracelet of clear, square-cut stones that glinted like blue diamonds.

If they were real, I judged that a similar bracelet for Fausta would cost me about ten years of my income.

The third couple consisted of a lean, debonair man of about thirty and a giggling blonde about eight years younger. The man was named Walter Ford and the girl Beatrice Duval. Immediately after introductions, the latter informed me I could call her Bubbles.

'Thank you, Bubbles,' I said. 'Call me Manny in return.'

Bubbles giggled.

It developed the sextet's celebration was in honor of a corporation formed only that day, and all four stockholders were in the party. Barney Amhurst was the newly named president, and Ed Friday, Walter Ford and the red-haired Madeline Strong comprised his board of directors. The lacquered brunette and the giggling blonde were not stockholders, it seemed, but were along only to round things out.

Barney Amhurst and Madeline Strong between them explained that the Hunt-safe Company, Incorporated, had been formed to manufacture and distribute an invention of Amhurst's which both fondly referred to as the 'Gimmick.' Apparently everyone else in the party, including Fausta, knew what the Gimmick was, but no one undertook to explain it to me. From the conversation all I could gather was that it in some way had to do with deer hunting, it worked, and it was going to make a pile of money.

By the time we had toasted our way through two quarts of champagne, I also gathered there was a change of plans under way among the celebrants. Apparently the original plan for the evening had been dinner and champagne in El Patio's dining room, then transfer to the ballroom, which is across the cocktail lounge on the other side of the building, where they could intersperse more serious drinking with an occasional dance. But someone, Barney Amhurst, I believe, suggested a private party might result in more uninhibited celebration, and the next thing I knew everyone was enthusiastic about repairing in a body to Amhurst's apartment.

As a matter of course Fausta and I were invited, and as a matter of course I politely declined. Not that we had any other unbreakable plans — we had already had dinner in Fausta's apartment and merely contemplated visiting a night spot or two, then taking a drive along the river road — but I felt we were being invited only as a matter of course, and I didn't want to intrude on a private party. But Barney Amhurst insisted to the point where he was almost demanding to know what we intended doing instead of attending his party, and Bubbles, who suddenly seemed to take an unexpected fancy to me, added her insistence.

When the waiter had brought chairs for Fausta and me, he had placed Fausta's on Amhurst's right between Amhurst and the debonair Walter Ford. Bubbles Duval immediately moved her chair away from Ford's in order to make space for the second chair, with the result that I ended up between her and her escort.

I sat next to Bubbles for several minutes before discovering, to my considerable surprise, that she was a rubber.

Another man would have discovered it immediately, for I believe her left calf pressed against my right almost the moment I sat down. But my right calf consists of aluminum and cork instead of flesh and bone, as that leg ends in a stump just below the knee. I am so used to wearing an artificial leg that it no longer impairs my activities in the slightest degree, but I have never been able to induce in it a sense of feeling. Consequently, it was only when she became emboldened by my apparent agreeability to having my leg rubbed by hers, and increased the pressure to the point where I was in danger of being pushed off my chair, that I realized what she was doing.

My first impulse was to shift my position, but then what Fausta refers to as my 'perverted sense of humor' got the best of me. Somehow the thought of what the blonde's reaction would be if she discovered she was wasting her caresses on an inanimate mechanical contrivance instead of a male leg struck me as funny, so I merely braced myself against the pressure and left it there for her to rub.

Momentarily letting up on the pressure, Bubbles leaned over and whispered in my ear, 'Please come to the party, Manny. We've got to have one live man there.' Then she glanced past me at Walter Ford, made a small face and giggled.

2

Catching this byplay, Fausta studied Bubbles momentarily with narrowed eyes, decided she wasn't important competition, and dismissed her. This was not because Bubbles was unattractive in Fausta's estimation, I knew, but only because she was aware I am constituted so that the only emotion girls ten years younger than I can arouse in me is paternal instinct. I prefer my women more mature.

Fausta studied Evelyn Karnes a little more thoughtfully, but since the lacquered brunette had not once glanced at me since we were introduced, or at anyone else other than Walter Ford for that matter, apparently Fausta decided she would not be active competition either. Evelyn could not seem to keep her eyes off Walter's sardonically handsome face, and her unconcealed interest in the man did not go unnoticed by her escort,

Ed Friday. Though he made no attempt to draw his date's attention back to himself, the way in which his teeth clamped down on the fat cigar he was smoking when he looked from Evelyn to Walter Ford and back again indicated his thoughts were not pleasant.

In a less open way Ford was returning the brunette's attention, which I suspect was the reason Bubbles so eagerly accepted my addition to the party

The third woman in the group, the red-haired Madeline Strong, Fausta did not even consider, as she seemed to have a friendly interest in the girl, and Fausta never mistrusts her friends.

Lest I create the impression that I am a roué and Fausta is a shrew, let me explain that Fausta's jealousy is a matter of habit rather than emotion. Years back, when she was a penniless refugee, we had a violent romance which nearly ended in marriage. But unfortunately I tend to be pigheaded, and from the moment Fausta started to gain success in the night-club business, I started to back out of the picture. On the old-fashioned theory that the man is supposed to be the breadwinner, the richer she became, the farther I backed. Now that she was one of the richest women in town, I had backed so far that we saw each other not more than once in two weeks.

Having completed her estimation of the situation, Fausta seemed to decide she was capable of protecting me from any of the women present, and gave me a questioning look. I passed the decision back again by shrugging.

'We will come for a little while,' Fausta told Barney, leaving herself an out in case we decided we didn't like the party. 'Manny and I have some plans for later on.'

As I already had my hat in my hand and Fausta was carrying her evening cloak over her arm, we stopped at the front door to have a word with Mouldy Greene while the others reclaimed various articles from the cloakroom. Mouldy, whose actual name is Marmaduke Greene and who derives his nickname from a mild case of acne, holds a position at El Patio rather hard to define.

During my stint in the army, Mouldy

had been a basic in the company in which I was first sergeant. According to army regulations, a basic is a private without a specialty, but it was a misdesignation in Mouldy's case, for he definitely had a specialty. His specialty was fouling up details.

I doubt that any army ever contained a less efficient soldier than Marmaduke Greene, and the few gray hairs I developed in service are directly attributable to his talent for doing the wrong thing at the worst possible moment. When the army finally released him with a sigh of relief, Mouldy got a job as bodyguard for the underworld character who at that time owned El Patio and ran it as a gambling casino. How he talked himself into the job is a question which has always intrigued me; for while he has a body encased in muscle, five minutes of conversation with Mouldy should have warned his prospective employer his head is encased in the same substance.

The result of this arrangement was a foregone conclusion. Louis Bagnell, Mouldy's gambler boss, failed to live out the year.

When Fausta took over El Patio and converted it into a supper club, it was already staffed with bartenders, waiters and a collection of bouncers, dice men and card dealers. She kept the bartenders and waiters, but cleaned out the rest with one swipe. When she came to Mouldy, however, softheartedness got the best of her judgment and she found herself incapable of casting him out into a competitive world.

She tried him at practically every job in the place, including headwaiter for one disastrous evening, before she discovered the job which was Mouldy's natural niche in life. Now he was El Patio's official customer-greeter, which involved his standing just inside the front door with a hideous smile on his face, greeting customers with friendly insults.

The more dignified the customer, the less formal Mouldy became. A typical greeting to a United States Senator might be, for example, 'Hi, Bub. How goes digging in the public trough?' Dowagers he invariably addressed as 'Babe,' usually accompanying the greeting with a resounding slap on the back.

Once new customers recovered from the initial shock, they loved Mouldy, for he had much the same charm as a friendly mongrel dog, if you can visualize a mongrel dog weighing two hundred and forty pounds.

Mouldy as usual greeted me as 'Sarge,' a hangover from army days; eyed Fausta's gown critically and commented that it wasn't a bad-looking rag.

'You going out with that old crook Ed Friday and his crowd?' he asked.

'Well, yes, but what makes you think Mr. Friday is a crook?'

Mouldy looked at her in astonishment. 'Everybody knows that, Fausta.' Then he said to me, 'Catch the big guy waiting by the door?'

Glancing that way, I nodded. The man was even bigger than Mouldy, though not as solidly built. He must have been six feet five, with heavy shoulders, and long, powerful arms. His eyes bulged and his lips hung slightly open, giving the impression he was on the verge of choking, but he wasn't actually. It must have been his normal expression, for he seemed in no discomfort.

17

'What about him?' I asked.

'He seems interested in your crook friend. Or someone in his party. He come in right on their tail, took a table near theirs, and after he finished eating, just sat there till they started out again. I been watching him 'cause I don't like his looks.'

'Thanks,' I said. 'I'll keep my eye out for him.'

When the rest of the group rejoined us and we went out together, I noted that the tall man left too. He was still waiting on the steps for his own car when the parking-lot attendant brought mine from around back and we drove off. In the rear-view mirror I could see him watching without any apparent interest as the other four in our party climbed into a taxi, and I decided Mouldy was having pipe dreams.

En route to Barney Amhurst's apartment I made conversation with the couple in the back seat by inquiring just what the invention was that was responsible for our celebration.

'We call it the Huntsafe,' Walter Ford

said. 'It's a portable warning device that lets hunters know when other hunters are nearby. The whole contraption weighs only two pounds and the transmitter, including batteries, is only one by three by four inches. It straps on the belt, and the receiver straps around the wrist like a watch.'

'I see,' I said dubiously. 'A sort of portable radar device. But is it efficient enough to sort hunters out from trees, or deer, or other objects that might reflect radar waves?'

'No, no. It doesn't work by reflection, like radar. It's based on the principle of the radio compass. The transmitter sets up a huge electromagnetic field around itself . . . a little over four hundred yards in radius. The idea is to get every hunter in the woods equipped with a Huntsafe. Then any time two hunters get within four hundred yards of each other, their receivers begin to tick like Geiger counters. The wrist receiver has an indicator on it resembling a compass needle, and when you hear the tick, you hold your wrist horizontal and the needle points straight at the other hunter. Then you avoid shooting in that direction. It's the most terrific thing in the field of outdoor sports in years. Do you know how many hunters are accidentally shot by other hunters every year?'

'No,' I admitted. 'But the thing isn't going to be very effective unless you can talk *all* hunters into buying it, is it?'

'Oh, we've got that figured,' Ford said confidently.

But he never got a chance to explain how, because Bubbles Duval, apparently tiring of being excluded from the conversation, changed the subject.

'Are you a professional boxer, Manny?' she asked suddenly.

'Me?' I asked, startled. 'No. I mean, not now.'

'You *were* though, huh?'

'Manny has not fought for years,' Fausta told Bubbles. 'He is a private detective.

'Oh!' Bubbles said in a thrilled voice. 'Like Martin Kane, private eye?'

'Nothing so glamorous,' I assured her. 'Most of my cases are insurance investigations, skip tracings or acting as bodyguard for people who think someone is mad at them. Mostly the last.'

'That's interesting,' Walter Ford remarked. 'We're practically surrounded by bodyguards tonight.'

He didn't explain the remark and no one asked him to.

Barney Amhurst lived at the Remley Apartments on McKnight Avenue, which is neither highly exclusive nor in a slum area. When we parked in front, the taxi containing the rest of the party double-parked next to us, and at the same time a gray coupé pulled to the curb directly behind my Plymouth.

While I was opening the door for Fausta, I glanced back at the coupé and noted its driver remained seated in the car. By the light of a nearby street lamp which cast a dim glow into the coupé's interior, I could faintly make out his face. Something about it seemed familiar.

Not being bashful, I walked over to the coupé and peered in. Its single occupant was the muscular guy with the hyperthyroid eyes who had followed us from El Patio.

'Anybody in our party you want to talk to?' I asked. 'Or are you just casing us for a heist?'

He merely stared at me without saying anything.

'I don't mean to be rude,' I said in a reasonable tone. 'But strangers following me around makes me nervous. Just give me a plausible explanation and we'll drop the subject.'

'Anything the matter?' asked a slurred voice behind me.

Turning, I found the reformed extortionist, Ed Friday, had come up and was watching us inquiringly.

'He was asking if maybe I'm going to heist somebody,' the man in the coupé said.

Friday chuckled. 'The misunderstanding is my fault, Max. I should have tipped Mr. Moon off.' To me he said, 'It's all right, Mr. Moon. Max is with me.'

'You ought to pin a label on him,' I said. 'Some jittery citizen might misinterpret his loitering and yell for the cops.'

Friday emitted a hearty laugh and slapped me on the shoulder.

3

Barney Amhurst's place was a four-room corner apartment on the first floor, its *décor* so overwhelmingly masculine it was obvious the effect had been striven for, possibly as compensation for our host's curly hair and dimples. Heavy leather furniture dominated the big front room, leather-bound volumes filled three rows of built-in bookshelves each side of the wide fireplace, and a mounted deer head stared at us from over the mantel when we entered the room. A rack of pipes on the mantel and another on a square end table drove the point home, and the whole effect was topped by a gunrack on one wall containing a deer rifle and a pump shotgun.

Wide French doors opened from the front room onto the outside lawn, with a step down of about two feet. When Barney led us into an equally masculine bedroom, where the men left their hats

23

and the women their evening capes, I noted similar French doors opened from there to a side lawn. A third room, presumably either another bedroom or a study, was off the front room, but its door was closed and our host didn't offer to show it to anyone.

The fourth room was a full-sized kitchen, into which Amhurst herded the men to assist in drink-mixing while the ladies repaired their make-up in the bathroom off the bedroom.

By the time we had gotten together eight highballs and transported them to the front room, Fausta, the red-haired Madeline Strong and the enameled brunette, Evelyn Karnes, had completed their repairs, but Bubbles was still in the bedroom.

'If we wait for Bubbles, the ice will melt,' Walter Ford said. 'Put her in front of a mirror and she's content for hours.' He raised his glass. 'A final toast to the Huntsafe before we settle down to serious drinking.'

Instantly Evelyn Karnes's glass was touching Ford's and she was smiling brilliantly into his face. Deliberately Ed Friday moved between the two, touched his glass to theirs and stared down at his date without expression. Evelyn's smile became mechanical as she hurriedly stepped back from Ford and made a point of standing close to Friday. The rest of us skipped touching glasses, signaling the toast merely by raising them slightly before drinking.

When we had drunk the toast, I said, 'On the way over, Mr. Ford explained to me what the Huntsafe was, but I didn't quite grasp its commercial value. I'm not trying to be a wet blanket, but what makes all of you so sure anyone will buy the contraption?'

Apparently this touched off the pet subject of the Huntsafe's inventor, for Barney Amhurst's eyes lighted with enthusiasm. Almost bounding at me, he stuck his finger against my chest.

'Do you have any idea how much money American sportsmen spend on their hobbies every year, Mr. Moon?'

I had to admit I didn't.

'Four billion dollars,' he said in an

impressive tone, spacing each word to stand individually.

The figure surprised me, and my face must have shown it, for he looked smugly triumphant.

'Of course that covers fishing as well as hunting, including the fees paid for millions of licenses; but if you deduct everything except the amount spent on hunting equipment, you still have a billion-dollar potential market. Know how many deer licenses are issued each year?'

Madeline Strong said abruptly, 'Does anyone want another drink?'

We all looked at her a little surprised, for no one, including Madeline herself, had consumed more than a third of the first drink.

Madeline reddened. In a low voice she said, 'I'll help myself, Barney, if you don't mind,' and departed for the kitchen while we were all still staring at her.

There was a moment of puzzled silence before Barney Amhurst said rather vaguely, 'I shouldn't mention deer hunting in front of Madeline, I suppose.'

This meant nothing to me, but apparently both Ed Friday and Walter Ford knew what he was talking about, for both gave understanding nods. When no one undertook to amplify, I broke the ensuing silence by bringing Amhurst back to the subject.

'Well, how many deer hunters do hit the woods every year?'

Immediately the inventor was all enthusiasm again. 'Deer licenses are issued in thirty-nine states plus Alaska,' he said. 'The total figure runs into millions. As a starter we're concentrating our sales approach on deer hunters, because most hunting accidents occur during deer season. But eventually we hope to educate all hunters into wearing Huntsafes.'

I was still puzzled. 'But unless every guy carrying a gun had one, it would be kind of useless, wouldn't it?'

Amhurst smiled at me delightedly. 'You've hit the key point of the whole idea, Mr. Moon. But that's Walt's function, so I'll let him explain it.'

He stepped back away from me and Walter Ford said simply, 'We're going to sell the idea to state legislatures.'

I thought this over, decided I got what he meant and said, 'You mean, get legislation enacted making the Huntsafe compulsory?'

Ford nodded. 'Make license applicants buy one before they can get a license. The thing is a natural. The annual casualty rate during deer season is appalling. The past season there were three hundred deaths from gunshot wounds and over a thousand other hunters wounded. State and local governments have been seeking a solution for years. I think we can convince at least the majority of state legislatures that requiring such a safety device is as logical as requiring brakes on a car.'

I began to see that this device was likely to be just as hot as the members of the new corporation believed it was. Added to Amhurst's and Ford's logical arguments, the fact that Ed Friday was involved in the project practically cinched that it was a good bet, for from what little I knew of the ex-racketeer, I was fairly certain wildcat speculation was out of his line, and that he wouldn't have come within miles of the new company unless he was satisfied it was going to be a roaring success.

It was not hard to figure what Friday's function in the corporation was either, now that I knew Barney Amhurst was the inventor and Walter Ford the man responsible for getting the product sold. Obviously Friday was putting up the money for manufacturing.

It was a little more difficult to place Madeline Strong in the scheme of things. I was still considering her without coming to any conclusions when she came back into the room. Her drink was at the same level as when she had left, which led me to believe she hadn't fixed herself another after all. Noticing me looking at her, Barney Amhurst gave his head a slight shake, as though warning me to let the subject we had been discussing drop in front of her.

I failed to understand it, but if for some reason deer hunting was a taboo subject in front of Madeline, I had no intention of violating the taboo. I stopped thinking about it in order to divide my attention between my drink and Fausta.

'Bubbles is still missing,' I remarked between sips. 'You strangle her while you had her alone in there?'

'Rubbing your leg so hard under the table probably exhausted her,' Fausta said. 'Probably she is taking a nap.'

I had not been aware Fausta had observed the blonde's strenuous caresses, and I thought it expedient to let the subject drop. Turning my attention to the room in general, I heard our host suggesting to Ford that they demonstrate the Gimmick for the benefit of Fausta and me.

A moment later Amhurst announced, 'Hold everything, folks. We'll be right back.'

Together he and Ford entered the one room we had not seen, leaving the door ajar.

Distinctly we could hear Barney Amhurst say, 'You take that set, Walt, and go back in the front room. I'll stay here and . . . '

He was interrupted by a tinkle of glass followed by the roar of a shot.

In the front room everyone froze to

immobility. Probably in a movie scene one or all of us would have rushed into the next room to investigate, but people don't react that way when a *real* shot sounds. I don't know what the others' mental processes were, but my first thought was that I wasn't carrying a gun. My second was a hope that Barney Amhurst, or Walter Ford, or both of them would step to the door and explain the explosion. My third thought, when nothing resulted from the hope, was a reluctant decision to push open the door and see what went on.

Probably less than thirty seconds elapsed between the shot and this decision, but these seemed like minutes because they elapsed in dead silence from both the front room and the room into which the two men had disappeared. I pushed the door wider, cautiously, ready to drop in case whoever had fired the shot decided to discourage curiosity by firing again.

The caution proved unnecessary.

The room into which I peered was a combination study and workshop containing a desk, a couple of leather chairs similar to those in the front room, and an electrical workbench running the length of one wall. Directly across from me were the inevitable French doors leading outside, in this case to the side lawn. They were closed, and on the floor in front of them lay a small pile of broken glass. A shattered pane near the center handle still contained a few thin shards of glass which had not fallen loose.

Sprawled on the floor to one side of the desk lay Walter Ford, his head queerly shortened and flattened because the top of it was missing. A good deal of blood had spattered over the desk, the floor and even over one wall.

Next to the workbench across the room from the body stood Barney Amhurst, a flat, boxlike object with a couple of wires protruding from it in his hands. His mouth was opening and closing soundlessly, like a fish kissing the side of a bowl, and he was staring glassy-eyed at the dead man.

'Amhurst!' I said sharply, but he didn't even turn his head.

When he continued merely to stare

fixedly at the corpse and talk without making any sound, I did the only thing you can do to snap someone out of shock quickly. I rocked his head to the right with a stinging slap across his cheek, then rocked it back the other way with the palm of my left hand.

His eyes focused on me, he gulped and said, 'My God! He shot him dead in his tracks!'

'Who?' I asked.

'The guy outside. Through the window. He knocked out the window and — my God, he shot him dead!'

His eyes strayed from me back to the corpse, he gulped, then suddenly clapped his free hand to his mouth and started for the bathroom at an unsteady run. I followed right behind him.

Everyone in the front room stared as we loped past them into the bedroom. Barney continued on into the bathroom, but I crashed headlong into Bubbles Duval, who had picked that moment to come out of the bedroom finally.

'Whoops!' Bubbles said, grabbing me around the neck to retain her balance.

She continued to hang on long after all danger of her falling over was past.

Reaching around behind my neck, I grasped her wrists, spread them outward and gently pushed her away.

'Sorry,' I said. 'Hurt any?'

The blonde shook her head and giggled. 'What blew up?' she inquired.

'The celebration,' I told her. 'We have a murder on our hands.'

Through the closed bathroom door I could hear Barney Amhurst retching over the bowl. Deciding he would keep for the moment, I shooed Bubbles into the front room. None of the occupants there had moved, but since Amhurst had thrown the door into the study wide in his headlong flight, two people were in a position to see the body on the floor. Ed Friday was gazing at it with a thoughtful expression on his face, and Evelyn Karnes was carefully avoiding looking at it at all.

Fausta asked, 'What happened, Manny?'

'Murder,' I said. 'Somebody outside knocked out a window and fired through it. Who and why we'll let the police figure out. I suggest everyone sit down and relax while I call them.'

Evelyn started toward the bedroom. 'Where are you going?' I asked.

The enameled brunette showed her teeth in a meaningless smile. 'I have to get up early. I'd better go home.'

Ed Friday's rubbery voice said, 'Sit down like the man said, you goddamned moron.'

His brutal tone startled everyone in the room except Evelyn, who seemingly was used to such talk from Friday. Without appearing in the least perturbed or resentful, she shrugged and obediently sat. Bubbles Duval broke the silence created by Friday's words.

'You said murder, Manny. Who?'

Everyone looked at her, but it was Ed Friday who answered. 'There were eight of us, Bubbles. Subtract the six here plus Barney in the bathroom, and you got it.' His tone was nearly as savage as when he had spoken to his own date, and I began to get the impression that for some reason he was furious over Walter Ford's murder.

The blonde's eyes swept over us one by one. Then she squealed, 'Walter! My date!' She looked at me with widening eyes and asked, 'Now, how am I going to get home?'

'For Pete's sake!' Friday remarked, and headed for the kitchen with a highball glass in his hand.

I phoned headquarters and reported the killing to Night Desk Sergeant Danny Blake.

4

Just as I hung up the phone, Barney Amhurst rejoined us. He was still breathing heavily but had regained most of his color and, aside from a rather dazed expression, seemed to have shaken off the effects of shock. I noticed he still carried the boxlike object he had been holding when I first poked my head into the study. He looked at it with a rather puzzled air, as though wondering why he was carrying it around, then crossed to the fireplace and laid it on the mantel.

'That part of the Huntsafe?' I asked.

Amhurst nodded. 'The transmitter.' Then tentatively he said, 'The killer, Mr. Moon. Shouldn't we . . . '

'Run outside to hunt him down in the dark?' I finished for him when he paused. 'No. He's gone by now, and we'd only trample any footprints he may have left if we start milling around in the yard. Besides, you have a gun?'

'Those.' Vaguely he gestured toward the rifle and shotgun in the wall rack.

'By the time we got those loaded, he'd be even farther away. We'll let the cops handle the search.'

Friday returned from the kitchen with a fresh drink, bringing with him a tray containing a bottle of bourbon, a soda siphon and a bowl of ice. He set it on an end table next to Evelyn, who immediately began to mix herself another drink.

To Friday I said, 'I'm going outside and bring in your bodyguard. See that no one leaves this room, and particularly that no one goes in there.' I pointed at the door of the murder room.

'Sure,' he said.

In the apartment house hallway several tenants were standing around discussing the explosion. When I stepped from Amhurst's door, they all looked at me.

'Somebody dropped a light bulb,' I explained.

One or two looked dubious, but they all started to drift back toward their own apartments.

The gray coupé containing Friday's

bodyguard was parked almost squarely in front of the building at a point where its occupant could not see the side lawn. Recalling that Friday had addressed the man as Max, I called him by name.

He was leaning back with his eyes closed listening to the car radio, and when I spoke through the open window, he merely opened his eyes and rolled his head sidewise.

'Yeah?' he asked.

'You see anyone come from the side of the building there in the last few minutes?' I pointed toward the corner of the building behind him.

Straightening, he peered over his shoulder. 'I ain't got eyes in the back of my head, mister. What's up? Anything the matter with Mr. Friday?'

'No, but you're wanted inside.'

When we entered the apartment together, Max looked at his employer inquiringly.

'Take your hat off,' Friday said.

Without changing expression the bodyguard hung his hat on the back of a chair, leaned against the wall next to the door and waited.

The first police to arrive were a couple of radio-car patrolmen. The elder of the pair glanced into the room containing the dead man, asked if anyone had left since the killing occurred, and when we told him no, advised us to relax until someone from Homicide got there. Then he picked an easy chair to relax in himself and simply waited, leaving his younger companion standing with his back to the door.

A few minutes later I was surprised when the chief of Homicide himself arrived. Usually Inspector Warren Day likes to forget his work after five p.m., and unless special circumstances or important people are involved, he leaves night calls to subordinates.

Day was trailed by his perennial shadow, Lieutenant Hannegan, who, as always, wore a plain blue serge suit which looked like a police uniform without brass buttons.

When Day was sure he had everyone's undivided attention, he swept off his straw hat, baring a totally bald scalp, and announced in the tone heralds customarily employ following a flurry of trumpets,

'I'm Inspector Warren Day of Homicide.'

Then, before the company fully recovered from this impressive performance, he swung his gaze at me. 'What are you doing here, Moon?'

'I was invited, Inspector. I was about to ask you the same thing. Doesn't Homicide have a night shift any more?'

'The chief was holding a department-head meeting, and it broke up just as your call came in.' He peered at me owlishly. 'When Blake told me you made the call, I decided to come over and see who you bumped this time.'

I said regretfully, 'Sorry, Inspector. Somebody else did the bumping.'

I led him into the combination work-room-study while Lieutenant Hannegan kept a watchful eye on the other occupants of the apartment. After kneeling beside the corpse for a moment, Day rose, glanced at the jagged hole the murder bullet had made in the plaster in the far corner of the room after it removed the top of Walter Ford's head, then turned his eyes toward the broken pane of the French doors.

'Walter Ford . . . that's the dead man . . . and Barney Amhurst . . . he's the slim, curly-haired guy with dimples . . . were in here alone when it happened,' I explained. 'According to Amhurst, someone outside smashed the pane and then fired.'

The inspector walked over to stare dissatisfiedly at the small pile of broken glass lying on the floor beneath the broken pane. 'Kind of a silly stunt, busting the glass first, wasn't it? You don't have to break the glass before you shoot through a closed window.'

'Murderers are silly people,' I told him. 'It happened the way Amhurst said, all right. The door into the front room was slightly ajar, and I distinctly heard the tinkle of broken glass before the gun went off.'

'Why were the two men in here alone?'

'They were getting ready to demonstrate an invention.' I started to explain what the Gimmick was, and how Fausta and I had happened to become involved in the celebration of the newly formed Huntsafe Company, then decided he would understand the contraption better if he got the explanation firsthand from its inventor.

Leading him back into the front room, I said, 'Amhurst better tell you about his invention. I'm a little vague on the details.'

'It's a portable warning device for hunters, Inspector,' Amhurst said. From the mantel he removed the transmitter he had placed there a short time before, moved a small catch, and showed that it opened like a box. Compactly arranged inside the case was a small square battery, a few things which looked like minute radio tubes, and a horseshoe-shaped coil wound with fine wire.

'This straps to your waist over the left hip,' he explained. 'About where G.I.s carry their first-aid packs.' He indicated the square battery. 'This is the crux of the whole thing. It's a battery of my own design and it develops seventy-five volts. Briefly, what the transmitter does is set up a huge electromagnetic field about itself. When another hunter enters this field equipped with a Huntsafe, the receivers of both hunters are activated. You wear the receiver on your wrist.'

In illustration he held out his left wrist, looked surprised to discover a compass-like object strapped to it, and said, 'I forgot I still had a receiver on. I slipped it on just as Walt was shot.'

Snapping shut the case of the transmitter, he flicked a tiny switch, set the case on the mantel again, and walked across the room away from it. When he was about ten feet away his wrist receiver began to emit a soft ticking sound. He stopped, held his wrist in a horizontal position, and the compass needle pointed straight at the transmitter.

'In the core of its own field the receiver doesn't work,' Amhurst said. 'If it did, its own transmitter would make it click constantly and the needle would spin in a circle. You have to be at least three yards from the transmitter, and it will work up to four hundred yards.'

'Hmph,' Day commented. He looked at Hannegan and ordered, 'Take a look around in there.'

While the lieutenant was carrying out this duty, Warren Day acquainted himself with Barney Amhurst's guests.

The inspector got no help whatever from either Ed Friday or his bodyguard, Max, both disclaiming any knowledge whatever of Walter Ford's private life. He did learn from Max that his last name was Furtell, but aside from that, his questioning of the two men was a waste of time.

From Amhurst himself, Day gleaned only the negative information that he would be unable to identify the murderer if he saw him again. Amhurst said he saw only a dim figure the other side of the glass, and could not even be certain whether it was a man or a woman. This was not surprising since it was pitch dark outside.

Reluctantly, the inspector turned to the women.

5

The red-haired Madeline Strong and the lacquered Evelyn Karnes were able to contribute nothing which interested Day either, but his expression grew alert when he learned Bubbles Duval had not been in the front room with the rest of us when the shot sounded.

'The dead man was your escort, wasn't he?' the inspector asked Bubbles.

'Yes, sir.'

Day walked into the bedroom where Bubbles had spent so much time. Through the open door I could see him cross to the French windows, unlatch them and stick out his head to peer toward the similar French windows letting into the study.

When he returned, he said, 'It would have been a simple matter to step out-doors from the bedroom, fire through the study window, and step back into the bed-room again.'

Bubbles shook her head. 'It couldn't

have happened that way, Inspector. I was in the bedroom the whole time, and nobody went in or out by the French doors.'

Day scowled past her at the usual forty-five-degree angle. 'How long did you know the dead man, Miss Duval?'

'Oh, ages,' Bubbles said. 'At least six weeks.'

'I don't think you can make anything out of that line of reasoning, Inspector,' Ed Friday put in. 'Ford hadn't been out with Bubbles more than a few times, and it looked to me like a casual affair for both of them.' He looked at Evelyn and said with a faint sneer, 'Ford was a great guy for casual affairs.'

'I thought you didn't know anything about Ford's private life,' the inspector shot at him.

Friday shrugged. 'There wasn't anything private about his relations with Bubbles. She's just a good-looking doll he dated when he had to appear somewhere in public with a date.' He stared at Bubbles with an expression which approached contempt. 'Besides, Bubbles won't fit for another reason. It takes at least a minimum amount of brains to squeeze a trigger.'

Bubbles giggled.

Hannegan came out of the study, looked at Day and shook his head.

'Nothing at all?' the inspector asked. The lieutenant shook his head again.

'Well, speak up!' Day blazed at him. 'Was the blasted room empty?'

Hannegan looked surprised. 'No, sir. You want a list?'

'I want a list.'

'Desk and chair,' Hannegan intoned. 'Pencils, stamps and stationery supplies in desk. A couple of file folders of business stuff and a few personal letters. None from the dead man, or mentioning the dead man. One waste can, empty except for a sliver of glass from the broken window. Two leather chairs. Nothing under the cushions. A workbench and cabinet with tools and electrical equipment. A rug. Nothing under it. Broken glass on floor.' He paused, stared at the inspector a moment, and then concluded, 'One corpse on the floor.'

'That's better,' Day growled. 'I didn't send you in there to gather material for your personal diary.'

A medical examiner arrived at that moment, and following in rapid order came a combination fingerprint man and photographer, two morgue attendants and three newspaper reporters. Before turning to deal with this influx, Day told Hannegan to take a look around outside.

I tailed along after Hannegan.

The lawn outside the study window was close-cropped and thick as a carpet, an impossible surface on which to leave footprints. Nevertheless Hannegan carefully shined his flash over an area several yards square around the French doors. When the light caught a shiny object just outside the doors, I stooped to pick it up.

Together we examined it under Hannegan's light. It was the casing of a twenty-five-caliber shell. I sniffed at it.

'Recently fired,' I said. 'It's the one that killed Ford all right. Must have been an automatic, since the casing was ejected.'

As usual, Hannegan said nothing. Taking a small envelope from his pocket, he held it toward me with the flap open. I dropped the shell casing inside.

Once more Hannegan methodically went over the area outside the French doors with his light, this time sweeping it in wider and wider circles. A good ten yards away from the doors the flash picked up a black object about six inches long. It turned out to be a short, curved pipe whose bowl was carved into the shape of a lion's head.

As the lieutenant dropped it into his pocket, I remarked, 'This killer left everything but an engraved calling card.'

There was nothing more to be found outside. We got back to the front room just in time to hear Day tell the reporters, 'I see this as premeditated murder. And once we've delved into the murdered man's past life, we won't have any trouble finding the motive. You can quote me as saying no stone will be left unturned . . . '

Jerry Thompson, the *Morning Blade* reporter, interrupted to say to me, 'You in on this case, Manny?'

'Just a guest at the party,' I told him. 'I don't know any more than you do.'

Day looked from the reporter to me and back again. 'As I was saying . . . '

'I think I've got everything I need, Inspector,' Jerry interrupted again. 'My deadline's in seven minutes. Thanks a lot for your co-operation.' And he quickly left the apartment.

The other two reporters slid out after him, leaving Day scowling after them.

Silently, the lieutenant handed him the envelope containing the shell casing and the pipe. After examining the former, Day handed it back. The pipe, he retained.

Turning to the group still gathered in the front room, he held up the pipe and asked, 'Any of you recognize this?'

He got blank looks from everyone but Barney Amhurst and Madeline Strong. Both of them looked faintly startled.

'Well?' the inspector demanded.

'I'm . . . I'm not sure,' the redhead said hesitantly. 'Where did you find it?'

In a more assured tone, Amhurst said, 'Of course you recognize it, Madeline. It's one of Tom Henry's pipes. He's a neighbor of mine, Inspector. Lives just two doors from here.'

'Does he now?' Day asked grimly. 'He in the habit of leaving his pipes on the lawn outside your study window?'

Madeline looked stricken. 'You must be mistaken, Inspector. Tom wouldn't . . . Tom *couldn't* . . . '

'Take it easy, Madeline,' Amhurst soothed. 'The inspector hasn't accused Tom of anything. And maybe it's just a pipe that looks like Tom's, and not really his at all.' In a candid tone he said to Day, 'I hardly think Tom Henry could be your killer, Inspector. I don't think he even knew Walt Ford.'

He looked inquiringly at Madeline, who said reluctantly, 'He only knew him slightly. Tom met him at my place once or twice.'

Amhurst favored the inspector with a winning smile. 'At most they were casual acquaintances, then. And murderers don't go around killing casual acquaintances, do they? Now if it was me who had stopped the bullet, maybe you'd have a motive, since we're rival inventors.'

'Let me get this straight,' the inspector said. 'You and this Henry fellow don't get along?'

'No, no, I didn't mean to imply that.

We're friendly enough. At least, we were once.' He glanced at Madeline with a discomfited expression. 'We did have a mild ruckus recently, but it didn't amount to anything.'

'Tell me about it anyway,' Day suggested.

Reluctantly, Amhurst said, 'A while back, Tom claimed my partner had stolen the original idea for the Gimmick from him. But after we talked it over, he realized the claim was silly. Inventors often find they have been wasting time working on some idea another inventor has already perfected but not yet announced. I guess Tom Henry actually had been experimenting with a device similar to the Huntsafe, but it was based on a different principle, and it was too big and heavy to be practical. He finally admitted he didn't have any claim on my patent. I've been kind of cool to him since, but I don't think he was particularly sore at me. He certainly wasn't sore enough to shoot anyone. And even if he had been, I should think I would have been the target instead of Walt.'

'Maybe he was just a lousy shot,' the inspector said.

As the implication of this remark sank home, Amhurst's eyes grew wide. He continued staring at Day until the inspector asked, 'Who is this partner you mentioned?'

'Lloyd Strong, Madeline's brother. He's been dead about eight months, but we started working on the Gimmick together. Lloyd died before we reached the answer. I only perfected the thing a month ago. But the original idea was his. It wasn't until after I applied for a patent that Henry dropped over and claimed Lloyd had stolen his idea.'

Madeline Strong's brother having been co-inventor of the Gimmick explained the puzzle of her interest in the Huntsafe Company. Presumably she had inherited the interest from her brother. However, nothing Amhurst had said explained the redhead's odd hesitancy in admitting she recognized the pipe. I got the impression she would not have admitted ever seeing it before had she not been certain Amhurst would disclose its ownership anyway.

Warren Day said, 'I think we'd better

make a call on this Henry fellow. Just give the address to Lieutenant Hannegan here, Mr. Amhurst.'

As Madeline watched Hannegan write down the address, her expression was a mixture of uncertainty and anxiety. Twice she seemed on the verge of saying something, but both times bit it off. Finally, she drew Fausta to one side, and began to talk to her in a low voice.

The medical examiner came from the study and asked Day, 'What is it you want to know about this guy? Time of death?'

'We already know that,' the inspector said.

'Then why'd you drag me away from a poker game? Any moron could determine cause of death. Somebody shot off the top of his head.'

'I know any moron could determine the cause of death,' the inspector said in a silky voice. 'That's why I called in a moron.'

The medic looked at him blankly for a moment, and started to open his mouth. 'I'll send you a report in the morning,' he said cautiously, and went out.

A moment later, the two morgue attendants and the lab man lugged the body away in a basket. They skirted the inspector widely as they passed.

'Doesn't it disturb your sleep to know you're such an ogre?' I asked him.

He peered at me over his glasses, started to snarl something, and then decided to ignore me.

'Just to eliminate remote possibilities, I want all of you people to submit to a search,' he announced generally. 'Hannegan and I will take the men, and if Miss Moreni is willing, she can search the women in the bedroom.' He looked at Fausta. 'I don't expect you to find one, but what we're looking for is a gun.'

No one objected to the search. While Fausta and the other three women were in the bedroom, Hannegan shook down Ed Friday and Max Furtell. Day went over me and Barney Amhurst. Aside from a small pocketknife in Friday's coat pocket, the only weapon which turned up was a .38 revolver under Max's arm. It had not been fired, and when the bodyguard produced a permit for it, Hannegan told him he could have it back the next day when Ballistics finished looking it over.

Bubbles and Evelyn came from the bedroom, smiled around brightly, and resumed their seats. Madeline Strong came next, and finally Fausta. She was carrying a small ivory-handled automatic in either hand.

'One from the purse of Miss Duval and one from the purse of Miss Karnes,' she reported, handing both guns to the inspector.

6

Ed Friday examined the sleek Evelyn with an expression of exasperation on his face. She looked back at him defensively.

'Just why were you lugging a gun around?' Friday asked.

'I'll handle the questions!' Day snapped at him. To Fausta he said, 'Which gun is whose?'

'They are initialed,' Fausta said.

Examining them, the inspector discovered each had tiny gold initials engraved on the ivory grips. Standing next to him, I could see that one gun bore the initials 'B.D.' and the other 'E.K.' They seemed to be about twenty-five-caliber guns, which was interesting inasmuch as the shell casing Hannegan and I had found outside was that size.

One at a time Day drew back the slides, released the clips, and peered down the barrels, sticking his thumb into the ejector slots so that his nail acted as a reflector.

'Neither fired,' he commented. 'You ladies got permits for these things?'

'I didn't buy mine,' Bubbles said. 'It was a gift.' Her tone seemed to indicate she assumed this relieved her of the necessity of having a permit.

'So was mine,' Evelyn chimed in.

The inspector handed both guns to Hannegan. 'Both of you be at headquarters at nine in the morning,' he grimly instructed the women. 'If the D.A. wants to overlook charging you with carrying concealed weapons, you can have them back after they're registered. But not to carry around in your purses any more. To keep in a drawer at home. Understand?'

Both women nodded agreeably and favored him with brilliant smiles. Neither seemed in the least disturbed insofar as the inspector was concerned, though Evelyn impressed me as being a trifle apprehensive about her escort's reaction. The inspector himself seemed more upset than either woman. Flushing at the overpowering smiles being directed at him, he doggedly continued his questioning.

'Where'd you get your gun?' he asked Bubbles.

'From Walter. Before he died, of course.'

Looking past the girl at a forty-five-degree angle, he asked, 'How long before he died?'

'About a week. No . . . two weeks. For my twenty-first birthday.'

Day neglected to inquire why Walter Ford had picked such an odd birthday present, possibly because he feared he might get another upsetting answer. Instead, he asked Evelyn Karnes to explain where she got her gun.

'From Walter also,' she said. 'A little over a month ago. For my . . . ' She paused, looked thoughtful for a moment, and went on, ' . . . for my twenty-fifth birthday.'

The red-haired Madeline announced, 'I've got one at home too, Inspector. Walter gave it to me for my birthday five months back. Why, I don't know. It struck me as a peculiar sort of present.'

Barney Amhurst emitted a cynical laugh. 'Not if you knew Walter.'

When the inspector stared at him inquiringly, Amhurst went on, 'All they cost Ford was the engraving. He was a purchasing agent for Maxim Electrical Products before he came in with us. He had dozens of contacts with supply-house salesmen, and to keep on his good side they slipped him presents now and then. Usually stuff they obtained at cost from other customers, I imagine, but some of the presents were quite valuable. They were also frequently impractical, but I guess Walt operated on the principle that you shouldn't look a gift horse in the mouth, because I never heard him mention turning anything down. I happen to know this particular present consisted of a dozen ivory-handled, twenty-five-caliber automatics.

'Walt hadn't a use in the world for them, but they're quite costly at retail, and made something of an impression as gifts. So he doled them out to people he wanted to impress. Women mostly, I think. At least, he never gave me one, and I had a birthday awhile back.'

Ed Friday said in a brittle voice to

Evelyn Karnes, 'Ford have some reason for wanting to impress you, baby?'

When she looked at him, for the first time her lacquered exterior seemed to crack, and a trace of fear showed through. 'Of course not, honey. I barely knew him.'

'I don't recall your mentioning him giving you a birthday present. I suppose you kept it to protect the present I gave you.' Crossing to her, he took her hand and jerked the diamond bracelet from her wrist. In a brutal voice he said, 'Now that you haven't got a gun to protect it with, I better take care of this.'

Her eyes were stricken as the bracelet, disappeared into Friday's pocket.

Warren Day broke the uncomfortable silence which followed. 'I want all you people to stay available until I tell you otherwise,' he said brusquely. Then he turned to Hannegan. 'Let's go see this Tom Henry fellow.'

As soon as the inspector and the lieutenant had departed, Madeline Strong said, 'Mr. Moon, Fausta tells me you're a private detective.'

I noticed Friday glanced at her sharply.

'Yes,' I admitted.

'If . . . if it proves necessary, would you handle an investigation for me?'

'What kind of investigation?'

'I . . . I'm not even sure it will be necessary. Could I call you tomorrow?'

'Sure,' I said. 'My number's in the book.'

The group began to break up then. Amhurst phoned for two taxis, one for himself to take Madeline home in, and the other for Friday and Evelyn. Bubbles seemed to take it for granted I was going to take her home, and attached herself to me and Fausta.

As I left with the two women, I noticed Ed Friday was deep in frowning conversation with Madeline. He looked up to call good-bye, and I was surprised to note an estimating expression in his eyes when they touched me, as though he were judging the ability of a potential opponent.

When we reached Bubbles' address, I thought it wise not to offer to accompany her to the door, and with equal wisdom Bubbles gave no indication that she expected this courtesy. The moment I pulled the car to a stop, she had the door open and was out on the sidewalk.

'Thank you, Mr. Moon,' she said primly. 'And I'm glad I met you, Miss Moreni.'

I'll bet, I thought; but all I said was that she was welcome.

On the way to El Patio I studiously avoided Bubbles as a conversational subject, and Fausta mentioned her only once.

'Miss Duval is a very attractive girl,' she said reflectively. 'She has the prettiest blonde hair I have ever seen on a brunette.'

Though it was only shortly after midnight when we reached El Patio, by the time we had a nightcap at the bar and Fausta had spread a little more goodwill by chatting with half the customers in the cocktail lounge, it was one o'clock and closing time. And it was nearly one-thirty by the time I got home.

As no garage comes with my apartment, I keep my Plymouth in a public garage half a block away. When, on foot, I neared the walk leading to the front door of the apartment house, I noticed a taxi parked directly in front. I glanced at it casually, then halted when a voice hailed me from the rear seat.

'Oh, Mr. Moon!'

As I walked over to the cab, the rear door opened and two men climbed out. One was Ed Friday and the other was his bodyguard, Max.

'We've been waiting for you for some time,' Friday said in a pleasant voice. 'Could I come in and talk to you for a minute?'

'Come ahead,' I said. 'I guess one more nightcap won't kill me.

Friday instructed the cab to wait, and both he and Max followed me up the walk, up the half-flight of stairs to my flat, and into my front room.

'Have a couple of chairs,' I said, and went on into the kitchen for ice cubes.

When I returned with a bowl of ice, I found my guests had made themselves at home in a couple of easy chairs. I mixed Friday a bourbon and water, then looked at Max Furtell inquiringly.

'He doesn't drink on duty,' Friday said.

I made myself a rye and water.

'Well, Mr. Friday, what's the important business that won't wait until morning?' I inquired when I was seated.

'I'd like to engage you professionally, Mr. Moon,' he said. 'I'd have brought up the subject earlier this evening, but I didn't realize you were a private investigator until just as you were leaving Amhurst's.'

Noncommittally I said, 'I see.'

'I had another man lined up for the job,' he went on. 'But about six this evening, he backed out on me. By then all the other private investigators' offices were closed, and I thought I was going to have to wait until morning to get a replacement. And morning is too late.'

'You mean you want me to start on some job tonight?'

'No, no, Mr. Moon. I merely want your commitment. I have to phone Mexico City at six a.m. and let them know I have an agent on the way, or the whole deal falls through. But you wouldn't actually have to leave until noon tomorrow.' He glanced at his watch and amended, 'Or, rather, noon today.'

'You want me to go to Mexico City?'

'Yes. I'm willing to pay a thousand dollars plus expenses, and the job won't require more than ten days. But first I'd better explain just what the job involves.'

I looked at him expressionlessly for a moment. Then I said, 'Don't strain your imagination, Mr. Friday. I'm sure you've thought up a nice convincing reason to send me to Mexico City, but I'm also sure that with your organization you could snap your fingers and any one of a hundred capable men would jump to do whatever needed doing down there. You don't have to hire an investigator whose record you haven't even had time to check. Let's cut through all the preliminaries and get to the real point. For some reason, you'd like me out of town for ten days, and are willing to pay me to leave. Right?'

It was his turn to examine me expressionlessly. Finally his heavy face broke into a rueful grin. 'You're more intelligent than I thought, Mr. Moon. Also a good deal blunter. I'll be just as blunt. Does a ten-day vacation with all expenses paid, plus a hundred dollars a day, appeal to you?'

'Naturally. But I'd have to know why.'

Slowly, he shook his head. 'We aren't going to be *that* blunt.'

'Let me guess,' I said. 'The first time you looked at me with any particular interest tonight was when Madeline Strong asked if I were a private detective, and suggested she might want to engage my services. As soon afterward as you could find me, you want me to leave town. The logical deduction is that you want to make sure I don't go to work for Miss Strong. Why?'

Friday's face had turned expressionless again. 'I don't plan to discuss any reasons with you, Mr. Moon. It's a simple take-it-or-leave-it proposition.'

'I'll leave it,' I said.

'Suppose we make the amount two thousand?'

I shook my head. 'Sorry. When you reach a million I might begin to waver, but for anything short of that, it wouldn't be worth it to me to go around with an unsatisfied curiosity. Up till now I wasn't particularly curious to hear what Miss Strong had to say, but now I can hardly wait until morning.'

Friday finished his drink and set down his glass. 'There are other methods I have found effective in bringing men around to my point of view, Mr. Moon.'

I said flatly, 'Is that a threat, you two-bit punk?'

Max Furtell was on his feet before I finished speaking. With a remarkably fast bound for so big a man, he was across the room and had jerked me to my feet by the shirt front.

I suspect all he intended was to pull my nose within an inch of his and advise me to speak more respectfully to his boss. But I have an aversion to being jerked around, even by men who outweigh me sixty pounds. I came erect without resistance, but I didn't stop my forward motion where Max wanted me to.

Instead, I smashed my left elbow into his jaw; and, when he released his hold on my shirt front, followed up with my right elbow.

Max took three involuntary steps

backward, stopped and blinked his eyes. Anyone with less than a cast-iron jaw would have fallen flat on his face after those blows, but all they did to Max was make him look momentarily dazed. He started back at me.

'Max!' Ed Friday said in a sharp voice.

The big man halted instantly, but continued to glower at me.

'This is ridiculous,' Friday said in a ponderous tone. 'I didn't bring you here to beat Mr. Moon up, Max. Apologize for attacking him.'

Without changing expression Max said tonelessly, 'I'm sorry I touched the punk.'

To me, Friday said, 'I can see this visit was a mistake, Mr. Moon. Shall we forget it took place?'

And, motioning his bodyguard to follow, he walked out without even awaiting an answer.

7

The morning after Friday's visit, I got up at my normal rising hour of noon, showered, shaved, and was diving into a plate of eggs and sausage when the door buzzer sounded. When I opened the door, I discovered my caller was Madeline Strong.

'Well!' I greeted her enthusiastically. 'Nothing sharpens my appetite like a beautiful redhead across the breakfast table. Come in and have some sausage and eggs.

'You will be looking at a blonde across the breakfast table while the redhead sits in a corner,' a firm voice said from beyond my range of vision. Then Fausta stepped into sight from where she had been standing to one side of the door.

In spite of her threat to make Madeline sit in a corner, Fausta allowed her a place at the table. Discreetly the girl chose one side, leaving the spot across from me to

71

Fausta. Neither accepted my offer of sausage and eggs, Fausta rather condescendingly informing me they had breakfasted four hours ago, but they did take coffee while I finished my breakfast.

When I was finished, Fausta said, 'This is a business call, Manny. Madeline wants you to work for her.'

'On something connected with last night?' I asked.

Fausta looked at Madeline and the redhead said, 'I didn't know what to do or who to turn to, Mr. Moon. I suppose I shouldn't have dragged Fausta into this. I guess I should have come alone. I phoned Fausta this morning because she's always been so . . . well, understanding. Maybe I shouldn't have bothered her. I really only know her from dining at El Patio, but there wasn't anyone else I could turn to for moral support. You see, my parents are both dead, and since my brother Lloyd was killed last November . . . '

'Whoa!' I cut in, realizing from the increasing rapidity with which she spoke that she was wound as tight as a watch spring, and unless I cut her off, she was going to take just as long as a watch to run down.

'Fausta has the run of this place. She pops in and out whenever the mood strikes her. Let's leave out the explanation of why she's with you and get on to your problem. What do you want me to do?'

She took a deep breath. 'Get Tom out of jail.'

'Tom?'

'Tom Henry. The fellow whose pipe was found on the lawn. They arrested him for Walter's murder.'

'I see,' I said. 'Did he do it?'

Madeline's eyes flashed. 'Of course he didn't do it. Tom wouldn't shoot anyone.'

'Then you don't need me,' I said. 'Contrary to popular belief, the police hardly ever frame innocent people. If he's innocent, they'll turn him loose.'

'You don't understand, Mr. Moon. They found the gun that killed Walter in Tom's workshop.'

'Oh.' I looked at her curiously. 'Then what makes you think he didn't do the shooting?'

Fausta answered for her. 'She is in love

with the boy, my thickheaded Romeo. And women in love have faith. They are not fickle like men, who will throw a woman to the dogs at the first whisper of suspicion.'

'All right,' I said to Madeline. 'You're in love with him, so naturally he is innocent. Tell me the details.'

It developed that there *were* no details beyond what she had already told me. Apparently, Warren Day had arrested the boy the previous night; and this morning, when he was allowed his one five-minute phone call, he had called Madeline instead of a lawyer.

It seemed to me that in five minutes he could have gotten across more information than the bare facts that the police had located the murder gun in his workshop and he was in jail, but after reflection I realized that a young couple in love might easily spend most of the five minutes assuring each other of their mutual love before getting down to less important business such as murder. Then I thought of something else.

'If you and this Tom Henry are so

much in love, how did you happen to be with Barney Amhurst last night?'

She looked at me in surprise. 'That was a special celebration. Normally Tom would have been along too, but you heard what Barney said last night about the disagreement he had with Tom. Tom doesn't hold any hard feelings against Barney, but under the circumstances he hardly felt like joining in celebrating the success of an invention which made obsolete the work he had been doing himself.

'I invited him, but he declined, and he knew I was going with Barney. Besides, Barney is such an old friend of the family, it was almost like being out with my brother.'

'What do you want me to do?' I asked. 'Make an independent investigation of the murder?'

'I want you to prove Tom didn't do it.'

I shook my head at her. 'No, ma'am. I don't take cases on that basis. If you want me to investigate the facts, fine. But any evidence I uncover bearing on the killing goes to the police, no matter where it points. If your Tom actually killed Ford, I not only won't undertake to prove he didn't, I'll do my best to prove he did. If you decide to hire me, that is.'

Madeline said, 'You couldn't possibly prove he did it, because he didn't. He told me so over the phone.'

While the girl dubiously thought over the wisdom of employing an investigator who promised to help convict instead of absolve her sweetheart if he actually proved to be guilty, Fausta said in a firm voice, 'Of course you want him to take the case, Madeline. Manny will find out the truth in no time at all. He is a very smart man.' She looked at me from narrowed eyes and added, 'Except about women.'

Madeline gave Fausta a trusting look and said in a small voice, 'All right, Mr. Moon. Can you start right away?'

'Immediately,' I told her. 'But there's a fee involved. Can you afford it if the investigation runs into a matter of weeks?'

She looked surprised. 'Of course. I have plenty of money.'

I told her my day rate and accepted a

retainer of fifty dollars.

'I'll start off with a question to you,' I said. 'Can you think of any reason Ed Friday *wouldn't* want you to engage me to check up on this murder?'

Blankly, she shook her head. 'I barely know the man. And I don't think Barney or Walter Ford knew him before about a month ago, when he came to Barney with an offer to invest in the Gimmick. Tom doesn't know him at all. Why do you ask that?'

'Just an impression I got,' I said. 'Quite possibly I misconstrued what he was getting at.'

8

Since the obvious place to begin my investigation was at police headquarters, my first stop was there. But before starting out, I cleverly instructed the girls to wait at my apartment until I returned so that I could give Madeline a complete report on Tom Henry's situation. I could just as easily have taken them along and had them wait in the lobby at police headquarters, of course, but I knew Fausta couldn't bear the condition of my flat very long, and I hoped if I left her in it a sufficient length of time, I would find it clean when I returned.

I like Warren Day and respect his ability as a cop, but if I may make my understatement for the day, his moods are unpredictable.

This particular afternoon I found my scrawny friend in a relatively equable frame of mind. He didn't fawn on me, but neither did he bite off my head for neglecting to knock before I opened his office door.

He merely gave me a sour look and said, 'I didn't send for you, Moon.'

'You have a young fellow named Thomas Henry in the pokey down here,' I said. 'Entered a charge yet?'

'Nothing serious,' Day said negligently. 'Just first-degree homicide.'

'Recall the red-haired girl you met last night? Madeline Strong? It seems she bears a deep and romantic love for your murder suspect,' I said, 'and believes the police have entered into a conspiracy with the real murderer to pin the killing on her Thomas. Naturally I told her that was ridiculous; that the Homicide Department wasn't dishonest, it was just inept. She hired me to do what I can for the boy.'

'That's nice,' Day said agreeably. 'Just offhand, the only thing I can think of you can do for him is hold his hand in the gas chamber.'

'I'm allergic to HCN,' I told him. 'I'd rather keep him out of the chamber. What have you got on him?'

'We went straight from Amhurst's place to this Thomas Henry's last night,' Day said. 'It's only two doors from Amhurst. Henry pretended to be in bed, but we pounded until he finally opened the door. The first thing we asked was for him to take a look at the pipe you and Hannegan found on the lawn outside the murder window. He admitted it was his, but couldn't account for it being on the lawn. While I questioned him, Hannegan took a look around. In a drawer in the boy's workshop, he found a twenty-five-caliber automatic like the ones the two women had. Only this one had been fired. We pulled Henry in on suspicion of homicide, and this morning changed the charge to homicide when Ballistics checked the shell casing you and Hannegan found near the pipe and decided the firing pin of Henry's gun had set it off.'

'How about the slug?' I asked. 'Did that check too?'

'When we dug it out of the wall, it was smashed all out of shape. A soft-nosed job. But its weight and composition were the same as the bullets remaining in the gun found in Henry's workshop. That, plus the firing-pin mark on the ejected casing, is enough to cinch it as the murder weapon in any jury's mind.'

'What's the motive supposed to be?'

'For Ford's murder? None. But remember the scrap Amhurst said he had with Henry because Henry thought he had stolen his invention? We think he was potting at Amhurst and accidentally hit Ford.'

'Maybe the gun was planted,' I said without conviction.

Day's grin contained the same type of enjoyment I imagine a fox shows when he has a fat rabbit cornered. 'That's what young Henry insists. Claims he never saw it before. But the gold initials on the grip read 'T.H.''

Dubiously, I thought this over. On the surface it sounded like a hopeless case, but I had to do what I could. In a way, the case was a little *too* hopeless, the circumstantial evidence a trifle *too* complete. And I kept remembering that Ed Friday had tried to bribe me to leave town for ten days, just about the time it would require to get Tom Henry properly indicted by a grand jury.

'May I see the boy?' I asked.

The inspector shrugged. 'If you want to waste your time.'

He pressed a buzzer on his desk, and after a moment Hannegan stuck his head in.

'Let Moon see Thomas Henry,' Day said expansively. 'He can have ten minutes.'

Thomas Henry was about twenty-five, long and gangling and with a mass of wiry black hair which stuck straight out from his head like the bristles of a scrub brush. He had a high, broad forehead, gentle and rather dreamy eyes, and a wide mouth which looked as though it was normally accustomed to a good-natured smile. At the moment, the corners were drooping.

He was seated on a drop-down bunk with his hands clasped between his knees when Hannegan unlocked the door, let me in, and relocked it again. Walking back down the corridor a few feet, the lieutenant waited impassively.

I told Henry who I was, why I was there; and, when I noted his eyes resting rather wistfully on my cigar, offered him one.

'Usually I smoke a pipe,' he said, 'But in all the confusion of being dragged to jail in the middle of the night, I forgot to bring one.' He accepted a cigar and, when I held a light for him, puffed cautiously, as though suspecting it might explode.

'To start out,' I said, 'I want you to understand you have to tell me the truth or I can't help you. If you killed Ford, I don't want a confession, but I want you to tell me to drop the case right now. There isn't any point in wasting Madeline's money on a lost cause.'

'I didn't kill him, Mr. Moon,' he said earnestly. He regarded me with a thoughtful expression and added, 'I don't much like the idea of Madeline bearing the expense though. Couldn't I assume the responsibility of paying you?'

'Got any money?'

'Well, no. A few dribbles of royalties from a couple of minor inventions. Nothing above living expenses. That is, not at the moment. I didn't mean I could pay you right away. I have a couple of new patent applications in, and both should bring me a lot of money within the next few years.'

'I may not live beyond the next few years,' I told him. 'Particularly if none of my clients pay me until their ships come in and I have to stop eating until they do. We'll let Madeline handle the bills, and if you feel indebted to her, pay her back when the bonanza arrives. Now, what's the story on the gun found in your workshop?'

He claimed he had never seen it before Hannegan pulled it from his workshop drawer.

'I understand it's probably one of several Walter Ford gave to various people as presents,' he said. 'I believe they're checking serial numbers to make sure. But Ford never gave me a gun. Why should he have? I've only known him a couple of months, and our acquaintance-ship was merely casual.'

'How casual?'

'Well, I met him at Madeline's house one night about three months ago when I dropped in unexpectedly. He and Madeline and

Barney Amhurst were having some kind of meeting. About the Huntsafe, I guess, though at the time I didn't even know Barney was working on the Huntsafe. After that, I saw Ford at Madeline's maybe a half-dozen times, but we never said more than a few words to each other. We certainly didn't know each other well enough to exchange presents.'

'How do you account for your initials on the pistol?'

'I don't,' he said.

There was nothing more I could get out of him about his relations with Walter Ford, but I did get his version of the ruckus with Barney Amhurst. According to Tom Henry, he himself had started working on a gadget similar to the Huntsafe while still a student at M.I.T. and had on several occasions discussed his idea with Madeline Strong's brother Lloyd, who was also a student there. Lloyd had never mentioned that he was working on the same idea himself.

'Lloyd was closemouthed to the point of secretiveness,' Henry said. 'You'd think that after I told him what I was doing, he'd return the compliment inasmuch as he was working on a similar project. Particularly since he was probably my best friend. I've known both Lloyd and Madeline since we were all kids together. But even Madeline didn't know what Lloyd and Barney were working on until after Lloyd was shot. You see . . . '

'Whoa!' I said. 'Lloyd was murdered too?'

9

Thomas Henry shook his head impatiently. 'No, no, Mr. Moon. A hunting accident last November. Up in the New York Catskills when five of us were out after deer.' His voice turned rueful. 'Kind of an ironic thing for a fellow who was working on an invention to prevent hunting accidents to die in exactly the kind of accident he was trying to eliminate.'

'What happened?' I asked.

'The usual asinine thing that happens too often every year when amateurs with guns fill the woods. Lloyd got himself in the wrong place at just the right time. He, Madeline, Barney Amhurst and I were out together. A girl named Beatrice Duval was along on the trip too, but . . . '

'Beatrice Duval?' I interrupted. 'You mean Bubbles?'

Henry looked surprised. 'You know her?'

'Last night, she was the date of the man you're accused of killing. What was she doing on your hunting trip?'

'She used to go around with Lloyd,' Henry said. 'What a fellow as intelligent as he was could see in such a dumb blonde, I don't know, but the last few months he was alive he dragged her everywhere. She had no business on a hunting trip. Beatrice is strictly an indoor girl. The first morning she went out with us, but Lloyd spent so much time untangling her from briars, it ruined the whole hunt. After that, she stayed at camp when the rest of us went out. Lloyd was killed on the third morning.'

'How'd it happen?

'I can tell you how, but I don't know why, because Lloyd was an experienced hunter and was used to hunting with that particular team. For the past three years he, Madeline, Barney and I had made the trip to the Catskills every fall.' He puffed thoughtfully at his cigar.

'Madeline and Barney were on a stand while Lloyd and I drove through a basin full of cedars. The basin wasn't large enough to get lost in, but somehow Lloyd got himself in such a position that when a buck broke from the cedars, he was behind it instead of off to the flank. It was nobody's fault but Lloyd's, because he knew where the shooters were and it was his business to stay out of the line of fire. Both Madeline and Barney fired at the deer, and both missed. One of the slugs hit Lloyd and killed him instantly.'

'Which one?'

Henry shrugged. 'They didn't make a comparison test of the bullet. Because it didn't really matter, I suppose. The coroner just issued a certificate of accidental death. Barney insisted it was his bullet, but I don't think he really knew. Madeline was so broken up, I think he just shouldered the blame to be gallant. In any event, it ended the hunting trip.'

'I see. Get back to your quarrel with Amhurst.'

'It wasn't much of a quarrel,' Henry said. 'One evening Madeline told me that Barney had completed work on the Huntsafe and had filed a patent application that day. It was the first I knew that he and Lloyd had been working on such a thing, because Barney had sworn all three of the other members of the proposed corporation to secrecy until the application was in. Madeline didn't know I was working on the same idea. Not that I deliberately kept it a secret, but Madeline doesn't understand electronics very well, and I just wasn't in the habit of discussing my work with her.

'When she told me about the Huntsafe, I got angry and went over and bawled Barney out for stealing my idea.'

I asked, 'Why do you say it wasn't much of a quarrel?'

'Because it wasn't. When Barney showed me the Huntsafe, I realized it was based on an entirely different principle than my invention, and made mine obsolete. Mine used an omnidirectional radio signal pretuned to a specific high frequency. In effect, it was a miniature broadcasting station, which automatically broadcast an intermittent signal. And its big defect was that, together with the receiver, the equipment weighed nearly twenty pounds. Amhurst's Huntsafe works on the principle of the radio compass and is powered by a seventy-five-volt battery he developed which is only two inches square and an inch thick. The whole outfit weighs only two pounds.

'After Amhurst explained it, I realized I was just unlucky not to have thought of the radio-compass principle myself, and my idea hadn't been stolen after all. So I apologized to Amhurst and went away.'

As I left headquarters, I mulled over in my mind whether or not I believed in Tom Henry's innocence. If I did believe in it, I had to assume someone had gone to elaborate lengths in order to frame him, for it was beyond the realm of possibility that mere coincidence could have woven such a tight net of circumstantial evidence. The evidence was so flawless, only one thing prevented me from accepting it at face value and deciding Henry was lying.

That one thing was Ed Friday's unsuccessful attempt to get me to leave town.

My reasoning was that I had been engaged by Madeline Strong to investigate the possibility of Thomas Henry's innocence, not to solve the crime, and I had no ethical responsibility to carry my investigation beyond that specific point. Logically, then, I had to start with the assumption that Henry was innocent, even though I was not at all sure of that in my own mind.

It followed that if he were innocent, Walter Ford had probably been the killer's real target, and not Barney Amhurst as the police believed, for it seemed to me unlikely that a killer capable of devising such an elaborate frame would make the mistake of killing the wrong victim.

I therefore began by looking into Walter Ford's background.

This led me to the personnel office of the Maxim Electrical Products Company, where Barney Amhurst had mentioned Ford worked before joining the newly formed Huntsafe Company.

It took me a considerable amount of explanation, a cigar for the personnel director and a phone check with Warren Day before I was able to get around the company rule that no information could be given out concerning ex-employees.

The call to Warren Day finally did it, but before the inspector would give me his blessing, he made me promise to let him in on everything I found out at Maxim.

'Have I ever held out on you?' I demanded over the phone.

'Yes,' he said.

So, reluctantly, I gave him my promise and handed the phone to the personnel director. Apparently Day was still in a sunny mood, for he told the man he could give me the same co-operation he would give the Homicide Department.

The results were even more gratifying than I reasonably could have expected, for Walter Ford's file was full of interesting information.

The most interesting item was that he had not quit but had been fired for using his position as purchasing agent in a racket which approached blackmail.

Ford had been caught accepting kickbacks, both cash and goods of various kinds, on orders he gave in the name of the company, the personnel director told me. An investigation subsequent to his discovery disclosed that he had used his power to approve or reject orders as a bludgeon to demand these kickbacks. He had been caught when he grew overconfident and tried to force tribute from a salesman who worked for one of Maxim's oldest and most reliable suppliers. Instead of coming across and receiving a plump order, the salesman reported the shakedown attempt to Maxim's general manager.

I also learned that Walter Ford had been married, though he was legally separated from his wife. According to the file, the widow was Mrs. Jennifer Ford at 2212 Wright Street, which was not more than a half-dozen blocks from the Remley Apartments.

From Maxim, I went to call on Mrs. Jennifer Ford, where I learned more interesting things about the dead man.

2212 Wright Street was a four-family flat, and Mrs. Ford occupied the lower left apartment. An attractive brunette in her late twenties with a sullen cast to her mouth, she came to the door wearing an ankle-length terrycloth housecoat.

When I had explained myself, she

invited me in rather dubiously and offered me a drink.

'This lad Thomas Henry has been arrested by the police,' I explained to her. 'I've been engaged to clear him of the murder charge, and I'm starting by trying to find out everything I can about your husband. I thought maybe you could help.'

'I can tell you in four words,' she said. 'He was a rat.'

I raised an eyebrow at her. 'In any specific way?'

'In every way.' She drained half her drink, fumbled for a cigarette from a small box on the low cocktail table in front of the sofa, and leaned forward to accept a light. Then she leaned back again and her sullen mouth blew a thin stream of smoke at me. 'He chased every woman he saw, and he was a liar, a crook and a blackmailer. He also didn't pay his alimony.'

'Let's take his vices one at a time,' I suggested. 'Chasing women, for instance. Any particular women?'

She smiled cynically. 'No *particular*

woman would have given Walt the time of day. He specialized in tramps. Recently, it's been a blonde dress model named Bubbles Duval and a chorus girl named Evelyn Karnes.'

I must have looked surprised, for she explained with a dismissive gesture, 'I've been having him tailed by a private detective. Trying to accumulate divorce evidence.'

Since the evidence could no longer be of any use to her, Mrs. Ford agreeably furnished me the name of the private detective, a man named Howard Quentin in the Bland Building. She also elaborated in some detail on her charges that her deceased husband had been a liar, crook and blackmailer.

'He got himself taken into this Huntsafe Company on out-and-out lies,' she said. 'He talked Barney Amhurst into believing he had all sorts of influence among state legislators all over the country, and wrangled a ten percent interest in the Huntsafe on the promise that he could get legislative action to make it compulsory. Walt was plenty smooth, too. He took the only two state legislators he knows, a New York State senator and a guy from Texas, to see Barney and have him explain the Huntsafe to them. Walt, of course, gave Barney the impression they were just two of dozens of contacts he had, and poor Barney fell for it.'

As evidence of his crookedness Mrs. Ford repeated what I had already learned from Maxim's personnel director about Ford's shenanigans as a purchasing agent. But what she told me about his black-mailing activities was brand new material.

He kept a file, the woman told me, con-taining compromising pictures of numerous women. Where he got them, she did not know; but she had once seen the file while they were still living together. As a matter of fact, her discovery of the indecent pic-tures had been the final factor in her decision to leave him. Mrs. Ford said she assumed at first they were merely bits of pornography he kept to gloat over pri-vately, but when she confronted him with the file, he laughed cynically and told her she would have a lot less money to spend if he didn't possess the pictures. Then she realized he was using them for blackmail.

She had one other minor bit of information I made a note of. The case of a dozen ivory-handled pistols had been obtained by Walter Ford while his wife still lived with him, and she was able to tell me it came from a salesman named Edward Yancy, who worked for a local wire-manufacturing company.

Before leaving the ungrieving widow, I used her phone to make two calls. One was to private detective Harold Quentin and the other to salesman Edward Yancy. Luckily, both happened to be in their offices.

From the former, I learned Walter Ford had surreptitiously visited Evelyn Karnes's flat on several occasions; and from the latter, I learned nothing except that the case of pistols had contained exactly twelve guns and they had come from another customer of his, the Tulsa Arms Company.

10

The hall door of my flat was open, and through it I could hear the drone of my vacuum cleaner. Cautiously, I entered just as the sound died away to a final wheeze.

Fausta, winding up the cord, stopped to look at me accusingly. She blew a strand of blonde hair out of her eyes, and I noted there was a smudge of dust on her straight little nose.

'You did it on purpose,' she insisted. 'You knew I could not stand to wait here in all this dirt.'

'You're even prettier when you're being domestic than you are in a green formal,' I said, walking over and bending to brush the spot of dust off her nose with a light kiss. 'You'd make some lucky man a fine housewife.'

'Hah!' she said, grabbing my ears and kissing me full on the mouth. Then she backed off in simulated outrage, as though I had attempted to attack her, gave me a light slap, and said, 'That is what you call blarney. No girl in her right mind would be a housewife for you. Who wants to stay home and slave while you gad about with other women?'

'The only woman I've spoken to since I last saw you was in the line of business,' I assured her. 'Where's Madeline?'

'If you are not interested in other women, why do you want Madeline?'

'I didn't say I wasn't interested in other women. I love each and every one of them. I just didn't happen to run into any who appealed to me while I was gone. Where's Madeline?'

'Where you keep all your women,' Fausta said sulkily. 'In the bedroom.'

At that moment, Madeline came through the bedroom doorway. She had a dustcloth in her hand and one of my dish towels tied around her head. 'That room is done,' she told Fausta. 'Are we all finished?' Then she looked at me.

'Hello, Mr. Moon. I hope you don't mind our cleaning things up. Fausta said . . . '

'I know,' I interrupted. 'Fausta said the

place was a pigpen. Believe me, I don't mind at all. Matter of fact, if you girls happen to be in the neighborhood about this time next week . . . '

'We will go by without even slowing down,' Fausta said. 'What did you find out about Madeline's Thomas?'

'He's in a jam,' I told them. 'Day's got enough circumstantial evidence to convict him right now. Almost too much evidence. If Henry is the killer, he's a lot stupider than he looks.'

I outlined everything I had learned, including my visit to Walter Ford's widow.

'I thought so,' Fausta said. 'Out carousing with a drunken widow while we work our fingers to the bone.'

Madeline said, 'That's the first I knew Walter Ford was married. Why, he even asked *me* for a date once.'

'I'm going to have to do some fast moving if I expect to pick up any defense evidence before Henry comes up before the grand jury,' I said. 'They sit next Tuesday. Madeline, I suggest you get hold of a lawyer for Tom in the meantime. You might also run over to his flat and pick up a couple of pipes and some tobacco to take him. Can you get in?'

'Yes.'

'Then I think I'll run you over,' I decided. 'I want to take a look at that neighborhood in daylight anyway.'

Fausta, whose workday did not really start until late afternoon, decided to come along too.

While Madeline and Fausta were hunting down Thomas Henry's landlord, I made a short study of the geography of the neighborhood. The Remley Apartments, where Barney Amhurst lived, was at 14 McKnight Avenue. Henry had a basement flat at 18 McKnight, just two buildings away. The three buildings — the Remley, the apartment next to it, and the one in which Henry lived — were surrounded by close-cropped lawn on all sides. As there were no hedges or fences between them, it obviously would have been possible for the killer to cross behind the center building as soon as he shot Ford, and arrive at Henry's door in a matter of seconds.

A check of the basement rear entrance

showed the lock was the simple old-fashioned kind which could be opened by a dime-store skeleton key. And when I peered through the window, I saw that this entrance led directly into Henry's workshop.

It didn't prove anything except that it would have been possible for the killer to plant the murder weapon as Henry insisted it had been planted.

After completing my geographic study, I decided to drop in on Barney Amhurst while waiting for the girls to finish whatever they were doing in Henry's apartment, but the visit was a waste of time insofar as finding out anything I didn't already know about Walter Ford and Thomas Henry. For no particular reason except that I ran out of other questions, I asked him about the accidental shooting of Lloyd Strong.

Amhurst's statement was substantially the same as Henry's, except that he admitted to me his belief that Madeline's bullet rather than his had killed her brother.

'The buck broke cover about two

hundred yards from us,' Amhurst said. 'Lloyd was about a hundred yards beyond it in a clump of underbrush. There was a slight upgrade from the buck's position to Lloyd's, and I'm sure I didn't shoot high. Just as I squeezed off the shot, I was conscious that I didn't have enough lead and knew that I had missed. But I'm equally sure I wasn't high. My slug should have hit the ground about halfway between the buck and Lloyd.'

'Why did you take the blame, then?' I asked.

'Well, Madeline was so upset over Lloyd's death, I was afraid learning she herself had killed him might throw her into a complete nervous breakdown. So I lied and told her I'd seen her slug kick up dirt in front of the buck just before I fired. She fired first, you see, but the truth is I didn't see her bullet strike anything.'

'Would it have been possible that neither of you shot him?' I asked. 'That the bullet came from another direction?'

He looked at me strangely. 'It's a funny thing you asked that. I had a feeling that when Madeline fired I heard another rifle crack at the same time, but I wrote it off as an echo. When nobody else mentioned hearing it, I decided it must have been an echo, but it still stuck in my mind. I suppose it's possible that some other hunter we didn't know was around accidentally shot Lloyd, but since from the law's point of view it didn't make much difference whose bullet killed him, I didn't see much point in confusing things by bringing it up at the inquest.'

I said, 'There wasn't any if Lloyd's death was really an accident.'

Amhurst's eyes grew wide. 'What do you mean by that?'

'Nothing in particular. But Walter Ford's death was definitely murder. And since four of the same people were in the vicinity when both men died, there is at least a possibility that the first death was murder too. I'm not saying Lloyd Strong *was* murdered, or even that I strongly suspect he was. But since we now know there is a murderer in some way connected with your little group, the possibility has to be at least considered. After all this time, I doubt that anything could be proved one way or the other, though.'

In an odd voice, Amhurst said, 'Since Tom Henry was the only person around when Lloyd was shot, aside from Madeline and me, when you start considering the possibility of Lloyd being murdered, you're actually considering the possibility of Tom having murdered him.'

'Not necessarily. Wasn't Bubbles Duval in your party too?'

'Not that day. She stayed back at camp.'

'You're sure? Ever bother to check if she spent all morning there?'

'Now you're being ridiculous,' Amhurst said. 'Why the devil would Bubbles want to kill Lloyd?'

'Probably she didn't. Probably she never left camp. But there is still the possibility. There are a lot of possibilities. Maybe Tom Henry shot him by accident and was afraid to admit it.'

Amhurst shook his head. 'If Tom did the shooting, it wasn't an accident. He and Lloyd were on the drive team, and when you're driving game you don't shoot. We had a standard rule about that.

When the party was separated, only those on a predesignated stand were allowed to shoot, no matter what kind of target showed.'

'There's another possibility too,' I said. 'Maybe either you or Madeline spotted Lloyd through the underbrush, took advantage of the situation, and deliberately shot him.'

For a moment the man looked at me. Then he laughed. 'Now you're really reaching out to left field.'

'Probably,' I admitted. 'The most likely possibility is that Lloyd's death was just what the inquest said it was. An accident.'

But in my own mind I didn't really believe that. Now that we knew there was a murderer around somewhere, it seemed a bit too coincidental for an earlier victim to have died accidentally. If Lloyd Strong's death had been murder, it bore all the hallmarks of as careful planning as the murder of Walter Ford. When I left Amhurst, I still was not absolutely convinced of Thomas Henry's innocence, but more and more I was inclined to regard it as probable that he had been framed. If he had, my task was to find the framer.

Though I knew of no motive anyone who had been present at Amhurst's the evening before might have to kill Ford, both Max Furtell and Bubbles Duval had opportunity. Since everyone else had been in the front room when the shots sounded, I could eliminate them as suspects. However, we had only the bodyguard's unsupported statement that he had not stirred from his car until I went after him, and only Bubbles' word that she had remained all that time in the bedroom.

The latter I tended to rule out because, while she would have had plenty of time to shoot Ford, step back into the bedroom through the French doors and then unobtrusively join the rest of us, she would not have had time to run across the intervening yards and plant the gun in Henry's workshop. Nor could she have planted it after she left, since Fausta and I took her home and she wasn't out of our sight between the time of the murder and the time Hannegan must have started his search of Henry's workshop.

Ed Friday's bodyguard easily had time to plant the pistol, though, since a good quarter-hour elapsed between the time the gun went off and I went outside for him. And for motive, all he needed was an order from Ed Friday.

The more I thought about it, the more possible it seemed that Friday had issued such an order. I was certain the ex-racketeer was capable of ordering murder if he thought it necessary to his plans, and equally certain Max Furtell would obey such an instruction. What Friday's motive could be, I had no idea, but I kept remembering his nocturnal visit to my flat and his attempt to get me out of town before Madeline could engage me to look into the murder.

I decided my next move would be to check into a possible relationship between Ed Friday and Walter Ford.

Madeline and Fausta had completed their mission of mercy while I was engaged with Amhurst, and were seated in the car when I came out. Madeline had in her lap a round, one-pound can of tobacco, and a collection of three pipes.

'You know some woman who lives in the Remley?' Fausta inquired.

'Several,' I said. 'And they're all mad about me. But I was visiting Barney Amhurst. You want to take that stuff over to Tom now, Madeline?'

When the girl said she did, I drove her over to headquarters and left her, then drove Fausta back to El Patio.

11

My next logical move should have been a visit to Evelyn Karnes in an attempt to discover just how far she thought Ed Friday's jealousy of Walter Ford might have taken him. While it was a little difficult to visualize the cynical Friday in an Othello role, he had exhibited jealousy of Walter Ford, and it was at least conceivable he had ordered him killed because Ford was making a play for Evelyn.

But Evelyn Karnes lived halfway across town. And since Bubbles Duval's apartment was only a mile or two from El Patio, I tried the blonde first.

It was pushing five when I left Fausta, and I stopped at the first drugstore I saw in order to use the phone. I found a Miss Beatrice Duval with a Dove Street address listed in the book, but there was no answer. Recalling that Mrs. Jennifer Ford had referred to Bubbles as a dress model, it occurred to me she might know where the girl worked. Mrs. Ford was at home, but apparently she had been pushing the gin bottle steadily ever since I had left her. In a thick, nearly incoherent voice, she told me she didn't know where any of her deceased husband's tramp girlfriends worked, and cared less.

As a last resort, I again phoned Howard Quentin, the private cop Mrs. Ford had employed to check on Walter's love life. I caught him, he informed me, just as he was walking out the door for the day.

He also informed me that Bubbles Duval modeled dresses at Saxon and Harder's.

There was a little delay in getting Bubbles to the phone at Saxon and Harder's, the store apparently being unaccustomed to having its models receive calls while working. When she finally answered, she sounded out of breath.

'Manny Moon,' I said. 'Remember me?'

'Of course,' she said with what sounded like a mixture of pleasure and misgiving. Then quickly, 'You better make it fast. We aren't supposed to get personal calls.'

'Sorry,' I said. 'I tried your home first. I want to see you. When do you get off work?'

'Tonight?'

'Yes.'

'Not till seven, Manny. And I have to get home to dress after that. Informal?'

'No,' I said, suddenly realizing she was misinterpreting my request to see her and thought I was calling for a date. 'You've got the wrong idea. I just . . . '

'My supervisor's heading this way,' she interrupted in a quick tone. 'Formal, then. But don't call for me. A couple of reporters have been hanging around trying to get my statement about last night, and they'd only bother you with a lot of questions too. I'll meet you somewhere. Where?'

'May I get a word in edgewise?' I asked.

'Oh, gee! She's looking right at me and tapping her foot. I have to hang up, Manny. Make it El Patio at eight.'

The last words came in a rush and were followed by a sharp click. Exasperatedly, I glared at the dead phone for a moment before slamming the receiver back on its hook. El Patio, the girl had said. It wasn't bad enough to be roped into a date I had no desire for, it had to take place right under the interested eye of Fausta.

Then I got sore at Bubbles. After Fausta's reaction the evening before, she should have known better than to pick Fausta's own club for a rendezvous, even though she was rattled by her supervisor's observation. If the girl was that empty-headed, she deserved whatever Fausta did to her.

And since I did want to talk to Bubbles, I phoned El Patio, got hold of the headwaiter and reserved a table for two at eight.

Evelyn Karnes was listed in the phone book at 1114 Grand. Dropping another dime in the slot, I dialed the phone number listed.

After a few rings, the enameled brunette's clear but lifeless voice said, 'Hello.'

'Evelyn?' I asked. 'Manny Moon.' Then, before she could get the same misapprehension Bubbles had suffered as to the reason for my call, I added distinctly, 'I'd like to talk to you for a few moments about last night. You going to be home for a while?'

'Until seven. I have a rehearsal scheduled at seven-thirty.'

'I'll be right over,' I said, and hung up.

Evelyn Karnes lived in the lower right flat of a four-family building. The neighborhood was moderately quiet and the building fairly new and modern. From the outside, it was nothing you might not expect a chorus girl to be able to afford, however.

But inside, the apartment was at a fantastically different economic level than the neighborhood. Evelyn's wages had never paid for the thick Oriental rugs, the deep-cushioned modern furniture or the luxurious drapes at the windows. The furnishings were fabulously expansive. The place was not a home, it was the love abode of an Oriental satrap. Everything in it was either soft or sensual, from the white bear rug in front of the fireplace to the excellent nude originals on the walls.

As she mixed drinks for both of us at the bar, I wondered what Friday saw in the girl. She was beautiful, of course, but the ex-racketeer's wealth could have bought him any number of beautiful women. Beneath Evelyn's beauty there seemed to be nothing: no humor, no conversational ability, no interests beyond the shallow interests of self. And, judging by last night, no personal regard for Ed Friday beyond a rather abject recognition of duty due him as her provider.

But apparently she possessed whatever it was Ed Friday wanted in a woman. I noted she again wore the diamond bracelet he had ripped from her wrist the evening before.

Sliding a rye and water across the small bar to me, she asked, 'Want to go into the front room, or stay in here?'

'This is fine,' I said, seating myself on one of the three slim bar stools.

'Okay,' Evelyn said indifferently. She stayed on the other side, leaning against the back bar and eyeing the drink in her hand with more interest than she had so far exhibited in me.

'Madeline Strong has engaged me to look into Walter Ford's murder,' I told her. 'I thought maybe you could give me a little background on Ford, seeing as he was such a good friend of yours.'

'Of mine?' She looked at me in surprise.

'He gave you a birthday present.'

'Oh, that.' She shrugged, took another sip and looked at me without expression. 'I guess he gave away a lot of those little guns. It didn't mean anything.'

'It did to Ed Friday. He didn't like it a bit. Anyway, I didn't mean just the gift when I said Walter Ford was a good friend of yours. Did you know Ford's wife was planning to name you co-respondent in a divorce case?'

She looked at me blankly. 'Me?'

'You,' I assured her. 'She had a private detective tailing Ford, and on several occasions he tailed him to this apartment. At least once, Ford spent the night here.'

Her body straightened haughtily. 'You're being insulting, Mr. Moon.'

'I frequently am,' I admitted. 'Sometimes it's hard to be polite when you're working on a murder case. Murder itself is not polite. So to get on with our conversation, Walter Ford was a good enough friend to spend the night here when Ed Friday was busy elsewhere. Right?'

Behind me a slurred voice said, 'Right, if it's any of your business, Mr. Moon. Now let's drop the subject.'

Swinging around on my stool, I saw Ed Friday standing motionless in the doorway leading from the front room. In his hand he held a door key, which he dropped into a pocket as I watched.

Behind the ex-racketeer stood his bodyguard, Max Furtell. Friday moved his thick body into the room and across to Evelyn, who came from behind the bar to meet him. Max stayed in the doorway.

Friday dipped his head to give Evelyn a perfunctory kiss, then turned to face me. Neither he nor the girl seemed in the least perturbed over his having overheard my remark about Walter Ford's clandestine visits to the apartment.

Correctly interpreting my puzzled expression, the ex-racketeer said, 'We had the subject of Walter Ford all out last night after I brought Evelyn home, Mr. Moon. He was a chaser and Evelyn was enough of a sucker to let him play around a little.

But the man's dead and I can't work up much jealousy over a dead man. As far as I'm concerned, the subject's closed.'

'It isn't your jealousy of dead men that interests me,' I said. 'I'm more concerned with how jealous you were of Ford before he got dead.'

For a moment he merely examined my face. Then he said in a quiet voice, 'I didn't happen to know about Ford and Evelyn until after he was dead.'

I cocked an eyebrow at him. 'I don't much approve of you, Friday, because I've got a silly prejudice against crooks. Even rich crooks who get their pictures in the papers for heading up charity drives. But I've got a lot of respect for your intelligence. Five minutes after I joined your party last night, I could see your date was carrying a torch for Walter Ford and he was playing her along for the laughs. I really don't believe you're so dumb you missed it.'

'I caught the play between them,' he admitted heavily. 'But I didn't know about Ford's visits here until after he was dead. What are you getting at? You got some fantastic theory dreamed up that I had Ford bumped because he passed at Evelyn?'

'It's a motive. And Max had plenty of opportunity.' When both Friday and Max snorted at this, I said, 'Don't bother to protest your bodyguard's unsullied virtue. You know and I know and Max knows that if you *had* told him to bump Ford, he'd have done it without batting an eye. Maybe he didn't kill Ford, but spare me your indignant protests that he's incapable of murder. I'd bet he's got at least six notches on his gun.'

Max made a growling noise deep in his throat. When I looked at him, he said huskily, 'Give me the word, boss, and I'll add a seventh notch.'

In a testy voice Friday said, 'He's just trying to needle you into saying something to bolster his empty theory, Max. Clam up. Don't even answer him again.' To me he said, 'I think you'd better leave.'

'Just when the conversation's getting interesting?' Draining my highball, I set the glass on the bar. 'Something else that's been puzzling me is why you were so eager to get me out of town. Since our single relationship had to do with Ford's death, I have to assume it was because you didn't want me messing in the case. You got some other explanation?'

Friday's face set in hard lines. 'I don't think I'm required to explain my actions to you, Mr. Moon. For your own good I suggest you get off my back and stay off. Max, show Mr. Moon to the door.'

'Sure,' the big man said with pleasure. He took a step toward me, but stopped when Friday said definitely, 'I said *show* him. I don't want any trouble in Evelyn's apartment.'

Disappointed, Max shrugged and politely moved aside to let me precede him. I was a little disappointed myself.

12

Usually I try to be prompt for appointments, but what must have been a subconscious desire to put off for as long as possible my meeting with Bubbles right under Fausta's nose made me linger in the shower longer than usual, have trouble getting the studs in my shirt front, and more trouble knotting a black bow tie. Then, at the last moment, when I was all dressed, had on my hat and was unable to think of any more reasons for delay, I decided it was my duty to phone my client and report what little progress I had made.

When I rang Madeline Strong's number, a man answered the phone.

'Is Madeline there?' I asked.

'Just a minute.' There was a pause as he apparently started to lay down the phone and then changed his mind. 'Is this Moon?'

'Yes. Who's this?'

'Barney Amhurst. I recognized your

voice. Madeline is kind of down in the dumps over Tom's arrest, and I'm over here trying to cheer her up. Hang on a minute.'

This time I heard the phone rap on the table as he laid it down. A moment later Madeline's voice said, 'Hello.'

'Manny Moon,' I said. 'Just thought I'd phone you a progress report. I don't want to get your hopes up, but it looks more and more as though any number of people might have had a motive for rubbing out Walter Ford.'

'Who?'

'I don't yet know enough to start bandying names,' I said. 'But I've got at least one fair suspect. And I may turn up a few more after I dig into Ford's black-mailing activities. When a blackmailer dies, it's always at least a strong possibility that someone he'd been blackmailing arranged his death. I really haven't as yet got any definite leads, but more and more I'm becoming convinced young Tom was framed. I thought it might make you feel a little better to know that.'

'Oh, it does,' she breathed into the

phone. 'You don't know how much better it makes me feel.'

'You get a lawyer for Tom?' I asked.

'Harvey Brighton. He's already been down to the jail to talk to Tom, and he's going to try to get bond set in the morning. If everything goes all right, Tom may be free on bond by noon tomorrow.'

I said dubiously, 'Did Brighton tell you that in a homicide case bond would run at least twenty-five thousand dollars?'

'Oh, yes. I can handle it all right.'

She said it so casually, I began to wonder just how rich she was. When I had asked if she could afford my fee, she had said, 'Of course. I have plenty of money.' That could have meant she had a million-dollar bank account, or only a couple of thousand. Engaging Harvey Brighton indicated she had more than a couple of thousand, because he was the state's top criminal lawyer, and I suspected he wouldn't even consider handling a criminal case without at least a thousand-dollar retainer. And now her implication that she could meet whatever bond the court set suggested her wealth was practically unlimited.

It occurred to me that I ought to dig into her credit rating before I made out my final bill so that I wouldn't make the mistake of charging too low a fee.

I said, 'I'll let you know the minute I dig up anything definite,' and rang off.

It was twenty after eight when I walked up El Patio's wide steps and was bowed through the bronze double doors by the uniformed doorman. Inside, Mouldy Greene failed to fracture my spine as usual with his catcher's-mitt-sized right hand. Instead, he merely examined me with puzzlement.

'You trying to commit suicide, Sarge?' he asked.

'She's here, huh?'

'In the dining room at the table you reserved. Fausta knows you reserved it, and she's been walking around with a funny look in her eye. Look, Sarge, it ain't too late. You go on home, and I'll tell this blonde kid you broke your hip and you'll phone her when it mends.'

'Thanks,' I said. 'But I'll take a chance on maybe getting it really broken.'

Instead of her favorite shade of green,

Fausta was wearing a turquoise-blue gown of some shiny material that looked like polished metal. It had even less front than her gowns usually possessed, exposing the upper swell of her firm breasts so far you could see the cleft between them; and where she was covered, the dress fitted as though it had been painted on.

As she swept toward me, she smiled brilliantly, with hands clasped in front of her, inclined her head the merest obsequious inch, and said with the formal politeness of a headwaiter, 'Good evening, Mr. Moon. Your young lady friend is already seated. Follow me, please.'

Cautiously I followed, keeping a discreet distance back in order to avoid any accidental contact between my good shin and one of Fausta's sharp heels. But apparently the caution was unnecessary, for her conduct remained impeccable. Too impeccable, I thought uneasily, as she made a graceful gesture toward my chair.

Bubbles, wearing a frilly gown which made her look about sixteen and made me feel like a grandfather, said with mock crossness, 'I thought maybe you'd stood me up, Manny honey.' Then she giggled.

'Hi,' I mumbled, stumbling slightly just before I took my seat. I thought about making some kind of excuse for being late, then decided: the hell with it.

'Is the table suitable, Mr. Honey?' Fausta asked me politely.

'Fine,' I said.

'Is your headwaiter sick tonight?' Bubbles asked Fausta. It was nothing you could put your finger on, but even though her tone was pleasantly friendly, Bubbles managed to insert a note of triumph into it. I am not sure how I knew, but suddenly it was quite clear to me that she had deliberately chosen El Patio in order to get under Fausta's skin.

Fausta said, 'The headwaiter is around somewhere. I often attend to favored customers myself. Sometimes I even cook for my best customers.'

Fausta slipped a menu into my hand, gave a smaller menu to Bubbles, favored us both with a bright smile and moved away.

Bubbles stared at the card in astonishment. 'Why, this is a child's menu!'

She held it up for me to see. Sure enough, it was the bill of fare El Patio made up for children, consisting of a number of colored pictures of animals, with the meals listed on the animals' bodies. The top one, I noted, was 'The Teddy Bear Special,' and included a small steak, half-portions of potatoes, vegetables and salad, milk served in a Mother Goose cup, and an ice-cream cone for dessert.

'She made a mistake,' I said hollowly, trading menus with her.

But I knew the child's menu had not been a mistake. It was merely Fausta's delicate way of accusing me of robbing the cradle.

Fausta brought the drinks herself, another departure from normal El Patio procedure, as I had never before seen either her or the headwaiter personally deliver anything to a customer aside from a menu. Noticing that the headwaiter was now back at his accustomed stand, I wondered if Fausta had now switched roles to that of waitress.

Apparently she had, for after depositing our drinks on the table, she went away and returned with a pencil and order card. Any of the regular waiters, of course, would have produced both from a pocket instead of having to go after them, but there was no place in Fausta's skin-tight ensemble to conceal even a pencil, let alone an order blank.

Bubbles decided to order spaghetti and meatballs.

By now I was too unnerved to put much thought into what I wanted for dinner, and settled for the first item on the menu. Unfortunately, I forgot I had traded menus with Bubbles.

'Teddy Bear Special,' I muttered. Then, when Bubbles giggled and I looked up to find Fausta was ignoring this and still patiently waiting for me to order, I realized which menu I had in my hand. 'I mean, a Bubbles Special. That is, the same thing Bubbles ordered.'

When our waitress had moved away, Bubbles said, 'You aren't engaged to Fausta, are you, Manny?'

'No. Why?'

She emitted a small giggle. 'You're acting like a teenager caught by his steady girlfriend out with another girl. Why don't you relax?'

'For one thing, I'm too old for you. You're only a kid. I'm thirty-two years old.'

'I'm twenty-one. Eleven years isn't too much difference.'

'It is for me,' I assured her. 'You remind me too much of my younger sister the last time I saw her.'

'You mean you want me to be just a platonic friend?'

'Something like that. We can confide our troubles to each other and weep on each other's shoulders over unfortunate love affairs. For instance, you could tell me about your affair with Walter Ford.'

'Walter? Whatever for? He's dead.'

'I know,' I said. 'Madeline Strong engaged me to investigate his murder.'

'You mean you asked me out just to ask questions about Walter?' she demanded indignantly.

'Not entirely,' I backtracked a little. 'Naturally, any man would jump at the chance of taking such a lovely blonde wining and dining. But working on the case gives me a chance to combine business with pleasure. You'd want to help me out if you could, wouldn't you?'

'I guess that would only be fair,' she admitted. 'What do you want to know?'

While I was framing questions in my mind, Bubbles took a sip of her martini, then lifted the olive out by its toothpick and started to take another. Suddenly she emitted a suppressed yelp, set down the glass and pushed it away from her.

In its bottom, where it had been hidden by the olive, was a dead fly.

13

An angry flush suffused Bubbles' doll-like face. As she started to open her mouth, I said rapidly, 'I'll order you another drink.'

'No!' Bubbles said decisively. 'She put it there on purpose. I'm not going to let that jealous female think she can get a rise out of me.'

Lifting the martini glass, she leaned over and emptied it into a vase of flowers bracketed to the pillar against which our table set. Removing the olive from the toothpick, she dropped that in also and returned the toothpick to the glass.

Holding my own drink up to the light, I examined it carefully, but could detect nothing floating in it except ice. Needing a drink to settle my nerves, I drained the glass.

A few moments later, a busboy deposited a tray of covered dishes on a nearby stand. Fausta, following behind him, nodded in signal that she would take over the serving and stopped before our table.

Eyeing Bubbles' empty glass, she asked, 'Was the cocktail all right, Miss Duval?'

'Delicious,' Bubbles said in a condescending tone.

Fausta blinked once, the only evidence of surprise she gave, then turned to the tray and began transferring dishes to our table.

As usual, the spaghetti was magnificent, but by now I was in no mood to appreciate it fully. Bubbles seemed to enjoy hers, however, falling to with a gusto surprising in a girl who couldn't have weighed more than a hundred and ten pounds.

During dinner I steered the conversation back to Walter Ford, but without learning a great deal more than I already knew about him. Not that Bubbles wasn't entirely willing to talk. The trouble was that she seemed to know remarkably little about the man. For instance, she seemed genuinely surprised to learn he had been married, though the knowledge didn't seem to upset her. She showed no particular concern when I told her Mrs. Ford had evidence, through a private detective, that Bubbles was one of the women Ford had been seeing.

'She can't name me as co-respondent in a divorce suit against a dead man,' she said philosophically. 'Walter and I were only casual friends anyway. He made a big play for me at first, but he had a wandering eye. And I didn't care enough about him to bother. I knew he was beginning to pant after Evelyn Karnes. You couldn't miss it when they were in the same party. Walt was all right as a man to go out with now and then, but I wasn't wasting any serious time on him. He spent money when we went out, but it stopped there. The only gift he ever gave me was that silly gun.'

'Bubbles, I understand you were on that trip last November when Lloyd Strong was killed. How did the shooting happen?'

'I wasn't there,' she said. 'I stayed back at base camp in the cabin. I think that was the day I painted my toenails.' She thought a moment, then said, 'Yes, I'm sure it was. I must have been painting them just about the time Lloyd was killed. I didn't know anything about it until hours afterward, of course, because the others went into town with the body and didn't get back to camp until that night. I went to the inquest the next day though. The coroner decided it was an accident and told us to go home.'

'And was it?' I asked.

She looked at me wide-eyed. 'Of course. You don't think Madeline shot her own brother on purpose, do you?'

By now we had both finished the entree, and my reply was interrupted by Fausta reappearing to take our orders for dessert.

When Fausta had moved off again and I had poured coffee for both of us, I said, 'I understood there was some question as to whose bullet hit Lloyd.'

Bubbles shrugged. 'Oh, that. Barney was just being gallant. He told me and Tom Henry privately he was sure his shot wasn't high enough to have reached Lloyd.'

I asked her how long Barney Amhurst

and Madeline Strong had known Walter Ford.

'For years, in a casual sort of way, I guess. I only met him about six weeks ago myself, but from remarks I've heard Barney and Madeline make, he was an old acquaintance of theirs. I suppose Lloyd must have known him too, though I never heard him mention Walter. I don't know how Walt got involved with the Gimmick, but I'm pretty sure Barney and Madeline weren't close friends of his until he became one of the company directors. You knew it was Walt who introduced Ed Friday to Barney and got him to put up the money for manufacturing, didn't you?'

'No, I didn't,' I said.

'Well, it was. Walt worked for Friday once about ten years ago.' She stirred her coffee thoughtfully. 'You know, it's funny I happened to know that, but didn't know Walt was married. I guess he wasn't in the habit of letting drop much information about himself.'

'He had a good reason. Did you know he had an interesting little sideline of blackmailing women with pornographic photographs of them that he had taken?'

She stopped her coffee cup halfway to her lips and slowly set it down again. A startled expression grew in her eyes, but for some odd reason I got the impression she was deliberately forcing it, and if she was actually surprised, her surprise stemmed more from my having knowledge that Ford had been a blackmailer than it did from the dead man's nefarious activities.

'Walt did?' she asked with patently false amazement.

'Among other shady activities,' I said dryly. 'His wife characterized him as a liar, a crook and a blackmailer. She also said he didn't pay his alimony.'

Fausta brought our dessert then, again interrupting the conversation.

'Was the spaghetti sauce all right?' she asked.

'Wonderful,' I said in a flat voice.

She didn't reappear again.

On the way out of the club I stopped to talk to Mouldy Greene while Bubbles visited the powder room. Mouldy was in typical form. Just as I stopped, a famous but aging matinée idol who was reputed to wear a toupee entered the club. Mouldy's face split into the terrifying expression he fondly believes is a smile of welcome.

'Hi, baldy,' he called. The famous stage lover winced, gave a hopeless shrug, and called back equably, 'Evening, Mouldy.'

Then El Patio's official customer-greeter turned to me. 'Still in one piece, huh?'

'I have a few inner scars,' I said. 'Where's your delectable boss?'

'Over there a minute ago.'

He pointed toward the archway into the ballroom, and I saw Fausta standing unobtrusively to one side of it looking toward us. When I crooked a finger at her, she came over reluctantly.

'For a grown woman, that was a pretty childish idea,' I said to her.

Across the cocktail lounge I saw Bubbles emerge from the powder room. Giving Fausta a cold look, I started to walk away.

'Wait, Manny!' Fausta called. 'Are you mad at me?'

Stopping, I said over my shoulder, 'Enraged.'

Moving up beside me, she looked up into my face and said in a small voice, 'Now you will stand me up tomorrow night.'

'I wouldn't dare,' I told her. 'I'd probably get a bomb in the mail.'

'You will be here?' she said, pleased. 'I will make it up, Manny. I will be awful good and not even frown when you smile at other women.'

'I'm sure of it,' I said dryly.

In a burst of generosity, she said, 'Why do not you and Bubbles go into the ballroom as guests of the house instead of leaving now? The first floor show will be soon.'

But, having watched all the performance I cared to for one evening, I politely declined the invitation.

14

I think Bubbles planned on making the rounds when we left El Patio, but I took her straight home.

It was only a little after ten when we arrived at her apartment door. She seemed a trifle chagrined that we weren't going to make a night of it, but not angry enough to stop crowding me.

'You're not much fun,' she said, wrinkling her nose at me.

'Old men usually aren't. What you need is some young hepcat with stamina.' I gave her a paternal kiss on the forehead and left her in front of her apartment door.

It was around ten-thirty when I slipped my key into my own door. As I pushed it shut behind me, I simultaneously reached out for the wall switch to my right. The result was that, when light sprang into the room, I had one arm out at a right angle to my body and the other behind me with the palm pressed against the door.

'Just hold that position,' said the slim young man who had been waiting in the dark in my favorite easy chair.

He couldn't have been older than twenty-two, and he had a thin, sharp-nosed face, its length emphasized by the lank black hair worn full across the temples in the manner of actors. Lips, oddly full for that long face, curled in a condescending smile. His dress was razor-sharp, and in his right hand he held a light blue Homburg.

In his left, he held a .22-caliber Woodsman Colt automatic.

I held my awkward position while he came lazily to his feet, set the Homburg on his head at a rakish angle, and moved forward to pat my pockets and feel underneath my arms. He held the muzzle of his pistol an inch from my nose while he made this investigation.

'Not heeled, huh?' he said, stepping back. 'Okay, you can drop them.'

Letting my arms drop to my sides, I examined him carefully. I had never seen him before, but I had met his type many times, usually in police line-ups.

He let me look him over thoroughly, a mocking light in his eyes, then said in a deliberately quiet voice, 'Turn around and open the door again.'

When I hesitated the barest fraction of a second, his trigger finger instantly began to whiten. The small bore was centered accurately between my eyes and the gun was steady as a rock.

I turned then, quickly but without abrupt movement. It wasn't necessary for him to elaborate orally, because that warning convinced me that if he didn't get instant obedience to his commands, he would put a bullet through my head without hesitation.

When he glanced past me and saw the hall was empty, he said, 'Start moving.'

I went out into the hall. Behind me, he switched off the light and closed the door. With my captor only a pace to the rear, I went down the half-flight of steps and outdoors. Usually I prefer a quiet neighborhood, but tonight I mentally cursed the location of my apartment house. The only person in sight was a half-block away and walking in the opposite direction.

'Across the street,' my abductor said.

Our destination was a dark blue Chrysler coupé parked directly across from the apartment building. He urged me around to the curb side of the car, which required passing behind it. For no particular reason except that I make a habit of mentally recording such information, I noted the license number was X-17-304-G.

At the gunman's direction, I slid under the wheel.

'It doesn't need a key,' he said. 'Just start it up.'

So much for my careful noting of the license number, I thought. No key being required meant a wire bridge across the ignition lock, which in turn meant a stolen car.

I examined the gun in his lap. It was pointing steadily at my right ear. 'You sure you've got the right guy?'

'The description fits and the right name was on the apartment door. There couldn't be two as ugly as you living in the same flat, could there? What's your name?'

'Reginald Walsh. You should see my apartment mate, Manny Moon, if you think I'm ugly.'

He gave me an indulgent grin. 'Just start the car, Mr. Moon.'

As he idly flicked on and off his gun's safety, I pressed the starter. 'Where to?'

'Head for the river road and turn north. I'll direct you from there.'

We had been moving in the direction of the river road about five minutes before I ventured, 'Any reason you can't tell me what this is all about?'

'Nope,' he said. 'Somebody who don't like you wants you out of circulation.'

'Permanently?'

'I don't think he'd care much. Not necessarily, if you behave. I got sort of free rein about that.'

I drove in silence for a few moments more, then asked, 'Decided whether or not you're going to make it permanent?'

He shook his head. 'You decide that. By how you behave, like I said.'

'And if I behave?'

'We just hole up for a couple of weeks. I hope you brought some money along. I like to play gin rummy.'

'Who is it that wants me out of circulation?'

'The chamber of commerce. They think you're an eyesore to the city. Now just shut up and drive.'

So I shut up and drove. When we reached the river road, I turned north as instructed and continued to drive.

We rode in silence for another five miles, then my guide abruptly ordered me to turn right onto a secondary gravel road. After a mile of this we turned into a dirt lane which ran about two hundred yards before it ended at an isolated cabin on stilts not fifty feet from the river bank.

'Park right under the cottage,' my abductor said.

As were most summer cabins along the river, this one was on stilts because of the annual spring floods. Beneath it was a carport just large enough to receive the Chrysler.

A wooden stairway led from the carport up into the cottage. Still under my captor's gun, I climbed the stairs. Just before we started up, he flicked a switch at the bottom of the steps which illuminated a small bulb at the top.

When I stopped before the closed door at the top, he said, 'See if it's open.'

Trying the knob, I shook my head. He handed me a slim key.

'This is a skeleton key,' I said.

'It'll work. Just open the door.'

The door had an old-fashioned lock, and the skeleton key opened it easily. Apparently my captor was not only covering his identity by using a stolen car, he was even using a stolen cabin. He seemed to be familiar with it, but the skeleton key made me suspect the place's owner had no idea his cabin was being used as a kidnaper's hideout.

The cabin's interior contained a large kitchen, two small bedrooms and a bathroom. The furnishings were about average for a summer place, mostly discards from some home. The stove was an old coal burner, as the place had no gas, but there was an electric refrigerator. It was ancient, but it ran when my companion turned on its switch.

Glancing through the open bedroom

doors, I saw that each was furnished with an old-fashioned brass bed, a double in one room and a single in the other.

'Not much to look at,' my companion said, 'but at least it's got electricity and running water. That's your room.' He pointed his gun toward the bedroom containing the single bed.

'You might have let me bring along a toothbrush,' I said. 'And am I supposed to wear this dinner jacket for two weeks?'

He snapped the fingers of his free hand. 'I forgot to have you bring up the luggage. I packed you a suitcase and stowed it in the Chrysler before you came home. Guess we'll have to go back downstairs again.'

He motioned with his gun, and I went back down to the car with him following. In the car trunk I found two suitcases, one of which I recognized as my own. Staggering upstairs with them, I dumped his on the kitchen floor and took my own into the bedroom he had indicated. He watched while I opened it on the bed and checked the contents.

He had done a good job of packing,

even remembering pajamas. In addition to toilet equipment, socks, shirts and underwear, he had included an old pair of slacks, a couple of sweatshirts and a light jacket, more suitable attire for a summer camp than the dinner jacket I was wearing.

Then, in the bottom of the suitcase, I found two pairs of handcuffs. All four links were open and there were no keys in evidence. Apparently, my abductor had the keys in his pocket.

'What are these for?' I asked.

'I found them in one of your dresser drawers,' he told me. 'Thought they might come in handy. Just throw them on the bed.'

Tossing the twin pairs of cuffs on the bed, I said, 'I can't just call you 'Hey You' for two weeks. What's your name?'

'Just call me Al, pal.'

I looked at my watch and saw it was now nearly midnight. 'Mind if I go to bed?'

'Suit yourself,' he said indifferently.

I sat on the far side of the bed with my back to him while I undressed and slid into pajamas. In that position, Al was unable to see that I had a false right leg. I didn't conceal it deliberately, because I am not sensitive about my missing limb. I just happened to sit that way. But as I slipped on the pajama bottoms, it occurred to me that quite possibly whoever had hired Al either did not know, or had not informed his minion, that my right leg is detachable below the knee. Thoughtfully eying the two pairs of handcuffs lying on the bed next to me, I decided there might be some advantage in keeping my infirmity a secret.

I kept my socks on, which effectively concealed the fact that my right foot is aluminum.

15

'Well, good night,' I said.

'Not quite yet,' Al told me. 'It's only a fifteen-foot drop from the window. I'm afraid you might walk in your sleep.'

Crossing to the wall, he removed the two sets of handcuffs.

'Stick out your left foot,' he ordered.

'I've got a boil on that ankle,' I protested. 'Don't go clamping a steel band around it.'

Shrugging, he rounded the bed and cinched the cuff around the ankle of my false right leg. He cuffed the other ring to the foot of the bed.

'You always sleep in your socks?'

'My feet get cold,' I said.

Rounding the bed again, he moved to the head, clicked one ring of the second set around my left wrist and attached the other ring to the center brass upright.

Then he put his gun away under his arm, said, 'Sleep tight, pal,' turned out the light and left me alone.

I waited what I estimated to be about fifteen minutes, listening to him moving around in the bedroom next to me. Then there was a creak of springs as he crawled in. I shifted position slightly and my own springs creaked.

Instantly, bare feet slapped to the floor next door. A moment later my door swung open, the light flashed on and Al stood there covering me with his tiny-bored Woodsman.

Opening my eyes, I said with simulated sleepiness, 'Now what?'

'Nothing,' he said, switching off the light, closing the door, and going back to bed.

Ten minutes later, I heard the rhythmic sound of snoring.

This time, I waited what I estimated to be a full hour before moving at all. Then I reached down so carefully that the old springs failed to creak at all, pulled up my right pajama leg and loosened the straps above and below the knee. When the stump was free, I slowly rolled over, set my left foot on the floor and pushed myself erect.

The ancient springs groaned horribly during this maneuver, but there was nothing I could do about it. Balanced on my good leg, with both hands gripping the head of the bed, I listened for some reaction from the next room while sweat trickled down the sides of my face. But Al's snoring continued uninterrupted.

My left hand was still cuffed to the center upright of the brass head, and without a hacksaw I could see no way to get it free. The only alternative was to take the bedhead with me.

Bending my knee, I reached down with my free right hand and felt the bed leg on my side where it touched the floor. It was equipped with a roller caster.

Rising again, I gripped the bedhead firmly by its center with both hands, first getting my left hand set while I guided the handcuff upward along the shaft it ringed so as to avoid the rasp of steel against brass. When both hands were in place, I pulled outward with gradually increasing pressure.

The casters were old and probably rusty. They resisted my efforts until my face was dripping with sweat. Then suddenly they responded with a squeal that raised my hair on end, and the bed moved out from the wall a good foot and a half. Simultaneously, I lost my balance and recovered it by planting my stump on the edge of the bed, which caused the springs to add their groan to the general racket.

Rigidly, I held that position, listening to the sudden and ominous silence from the next room. Al's bedsprings creaked as he shifted restlessly. Then I began to breathe again as his snoring resumed.

Still, I held my uncomfortable position for a full ten minutes before again daring to move. Then I risked another slight creak by regaining my one-legged stance alongside the bed. Steadying myself by hanging onto the bedhead with my left hand, I gripped the underside of the bedframe with my right and lifted. With only a slight rasping noise, the frame lifted out of the slot attaching it to the head. When I let it down again, that side sagged but did not touch the floor because the left side of the frame was still joined to the head.

Holding the handcuff chain with my right hand to prevent its rattling, I squeezed myself between the wall and the bed to the other side. There I repeated the operation, but this time when I let down the frame, it rested on the floor and the head was free.

Inevitably this created some noise. As usual the bed springs creaked, there was a loud thump when I let the frame down a trifle harder than I intended, and the casters squealed when the head started to slide and almost crashed into the wall.

I managed to steady it, however, and stood with my heart pounding, listening for sounds from Al.

Again the snoring had stopped.

I stood stock still, balanced on one foot with my shoulder against the wall and both hands steadying the brass head of the bed. But this time the snoring did not resume. Instead, I heard bare feet slap on the floor.

Desperately, I drew my lungs full of air and emitted it slowly in what I hoped sounded like a gentle snore. When there was no immediate further sound from the next room, I repeated the snore, then repeated it again.

To my tremendous relief I heard Al roll back into bed. But my relief wasn't so great that it made me reckless. I continued to issue a gentle snoring sound until it was drowned out by the real snores from Al's bedroom.

I waited a full quarter-hour before chancing another move. Then I lifted the light brass head completely off the floor, my heart moving to my mouth when the casters came loose and dropped to the floor with twin rattles. But when Al's snoring continued uninterrupted, I was glad to be rid of the caster's squeals.

Pulling the brass head under my left armpit, I used it as a cumbersome crutch. It was not heavy, being of hollow brass tubing, and it worked with remarkable efficiency. If Al had decided to put me in the double bed instead of the single one, I don't think I could have managed, because using the head of a double bed as a crutch would have been too awkward. But the single one made a fine walking aid.

Nevertheless, it took me nearly ten minutes to reach the door of my room, for with each step I had to bring the legs of my improvised crutch down softly while I precariously balanced on one leg, and I had to make sure they were firmly set on the floor and would not slide before I made another hop forward. In between hops, I listened for indications that Al might be awakened by my movements.

Getting through the door was difficult, and getting through Al's door into his bedroom required even more skill, for it was narrower. But somehow I managed it.

Fortunately, Al didn't awaken until I was nearly to his bedside.

Then he sat up abruptly, stared at me in the moonlight filtering through his window, and started to thrust his hand under his pillow.

Bracing myself on my brass crutch, I swung my leg forward and planted my foot in the center of his chest.

He went backward as though shot from a catapult, hit the open window and went through it, taking the screen with him.

Below, I heard the breaking of branches as he passed through a tree just outside the window on the way down.

Clambering off the bed, I got my crutch under my arm again and felt beneath Al's pillow for his gun. With it in my hand, I made my way to the wall where his suit hung, and then had to thrust the gun under the cord of my pajamas in order to have a free hand with which to search for the handcuff keys. I found them in a side pocket of his coat.

Altogether, a good five minutes passed before I was free of the brass anchor I had been carrying around and could hop to the window with the gun in my hand. Below, I could see no sign of my recent captor. As I studied the moonlit terrain with puzzlement, I heard the car start.

The carport opened on the kitchen side of the cabin, but before I could hop to the kitchen window, steadying myself against the walls and pieces of furniture as I went, the car had backed out and roared away up the dirt lane.

It was small satisfaction to know Al had been forced to drive off wearing only pajamas, for he had left me stranded miles from nowhere. And the cabin had no telephone.

The first thing I did was return to my bedroom to free my artificial leg from the grip of the second handcuff and strap it back on. Then I dressed in slacks, sweatshirt and jacket, packed my tuxedo in the suitcase, and set the suitcase on the kitchen table.

Then I went through the clothing Al had left behind.

There was nothing of interest in his suitcase except that all his underwear and socks were silk. But his wallet, which I found in the hip pocket of his trousers, gave at least a limited amount of information about him.

According to a driver's license in it, his legal name was Alberto Toma, he was barely twenty-one instead of the twenty-two I had guessed, his occupation was 'salesman', and his home address 1812 Sixth Street. I suspected that might be his actual address, since it was in the heart of the slum area which bred most of our local racketeers.

There was no point in sticking around the cabin any more. Checking the money compartment of the wallet, I discovered it contained slightly over two hundred dollars, mostly in twenties. I thrust the wallet into my pocket. The Woodsman I stuck under my belt beneath the jacket, then picked up my suitcase, turned out the lights and left.

It was four o'clock in the morning by the time I had walked as far as the river road, and four-thirty before I reached an all-night service station which had a phone. A taxi from town arrived for me forty-five minutes later, and it was six before I finally reached my apartment.

Setting my alarm for three hours later, I collapsed into bed.

16

At ten o'clock the next morning I walked into Warren Day's office. The inspector examined the circles under my eyes curiously before he spoke.

Then he said, 'This is police headquarters, Moon. You get transfusions over at City Hospital.'

'I only had three hours' sleep,' I announced.

'After-hours joints again, eh? If you'd have sense enough to go home when the legitimate bars close . . . '

I interrupted him by tossing Alberto Toma's wallet on his desk. 'I'd like a receipt for that. Particularly for the two hundred plus bucks in it. According to the driver's license, he's Alberto Toma and lives at 1812 Sixth. There's a chance that's his real name and address. In case it isn't, I'd like to look through the Wanted file.'

The inspector opened the wallet,

shuffled through the papers in it, scowled at me and wrote out a receipt. As I stuffed it into my pocket, he leaned back in his chair, clasped his hands over his lean stomach, and silently waited for me to get to the point.

Removing the Woodsman from under my belt, I shoved it across to him. 'This goes with the wallet. I'm almost sure it won't be registered, but maybe ballistic tests will tie it in with some unsolved killing or other.'

'Alberto's that kind of boy, eh?'

'He's that kind of boy,' I agreed. 'When I last saw him he was driving a dark blue Chrysler coupé, license number X-17-304-G, and was dressed only in pajamas. I think the coupé was stolen, and he's probably ditched it by now. He's also probably dug himself up some clothes. I'm just giving you this information for what it's worth.'

'Nothing you've said so far is worth much,' the inspector said. 'Just why would I be interested in this Alberto?'

'Among other things, he's a kidnaper,' I told him. And, briefly, I outlined my experience of the night before.

When I finished, Day carefully searched his ash tray for a cigar butt of sufficient length to suit him, blew it free of ash when he found one, and popped it into a corner of his mouth.

After silently chewing the already-frayed end for a moment, he said, 'Usually you don't waste my time, Moon, but aren't you in the wrong office? I've got enough worries running Homicide without piddling around with kidnapers.'

'This kidnaping has a bearing on a homicide,' I assured him. 'Whoever hired Alberto to get me out of the way did it to stop my looking into the Ford murder.'

The inspector looked dissatisfied. 'That's just a guess. Maybe you've been stepping on somebody's toes in some other case.'

'You don't want to concede the point because it louses up your nice case against Tom Henry,' I said. 'If someone is interested enough to resort to kidnaping to prevent my digging any farther into Ford's murder, it means Henry was framed.'

Passing his hand irritably over his scalp from rear to front — in a gesture which would have left his hair a mess, had he possessed any — he said in a weary tone, 'All right, Moon. I'll put out a call for this boy, and we'll ask him questions about Ford when we net him. Just where was this cabin he took you to?'

When I had described the location as best I could, he lifted his phone, relayed the information to someone, and instructed him to chase down the cabin's ownership. He also read off the Chrysler's license number to check.

Then he shooed me off to the record room, where, after a mere ten minutes of gazing at pictures of men whose descriptions conformed generally to that of my kidnaper, I located my man. It was not a hard search because he had not bothered to change his original name much. It was Alberto Thomaso, and in his short twenty-one years he had managed to accumulate a record of twelve arrests.

Returning to Day's office, I flipped the card in front of him.

'Lovable child, isn't he?' he grunted after reading the record.

Lifting his phone, he sent out a pickup

call on Alberto Thomaso, alias Alberto Toma.

When I resumed the same chair I had occupied previously, and showed no signs of leaving, Day scowled at me inquiringly.

'Now that we've decided my client is innocent, how about bringing me up to date on developments?' I suggested.

His scowl deepened. 'We've decided no such thing, Moon. I'm merely exercising an open mind.'

'Well, how about exercising it some more by letting me know what you've uncovered?'

The inspector grumbled a bit, but I think it was just to keep in practice. Despite what I considered a rather unreasonable insistence that his case against Tom Henry remained as strong as ever, I believe the kidnaping convinced him there actually was a probability Henry had been framed, and he was not at all averse to having me do some of the legwork a reinvestigation of the case would involve. An additional man working for him at no expense to the taxpayer was a bargain he had no intention of passing up. And, though his attitude was that he was doing me an exceptional favor by bringing me up to date, I suspect that even as he talked to me one part of his mind was secretly considering where he could best use the cop I would release.

A routine check had been made of Walter Ford's apartment, he told me. The case of twenty-five-caliber automatics had been located there, five of the original dozen still remaining, none of those being initialed. Six of the seven missing ones had been accounted for. In addition to the pistols Ford had given Madeline Strong, Bubbles Duval and Evelyn Karnes, two other female recipients had been located through an address book found in Ford's apartment. Both women claimed not to have seen Ford in weeks, and both had unshakable alibis for the time of the murder.

The sixth gun was the one found in Tom Henry's workshop drawer.

'That leaves one still floating around somewhere,' I remarked.

The inspector shrugged. 'Probably turn out he gave it to some woman who isn't listed in the address book.'

I said, 'Has it occurred to you as a bit odd that all the pistols Ford gave away were given to women, except for Tom Henry's? Why would a woman chaser like Ford make a gift to a man he barely knew, when he didn't customarily give presents to even his closest male friends?'

'I can't say, but there's evidence he actually did make the gift. In the first place, we traced the guns to the Tulsa Arms Company, and the serial number on Henry's gun proves it was one of the original dozen. In the second place, we located the jeweler who did Ford's engraving for him. Jessup's, over on West Lucas. It was Ford who ordered the 'T.H.' initials on young Henry's gun all right, just as he ordered the engraving on the other five initialed guns.'

'Only five? You mean the missing seventh gun was never engraved?'

Day shook his head. 'Not at Jessup's anyway. If it had been, we'd have located whoever Ford gave it to by now.'

I said thoughtfully, 'Offhand, it looks like that seventh gun was never given away. Ford would hardly break his habit of having them engraved.'

'Maybe it was the first one he gave as a present, and it didn't occur to him to start having initials engraved on the grips until he got to the second.' He paused a moment and added reluctantly, 'Except for something Hannegan said.'

'Hannegan said something? It must have been important to make the lieutenant open his mouth.'

'Just one of those odd things nobody but Hannegan would notice,' the inspector said. 'I doubt that it means anything. This gun case is a velvet-lined box, with velvet-covered spring clips that clamp around the barrel of each pistol to hold it in place. The guns were in three rows of four each. According to Tulsa, the twelve serial numbers were consecutive, and they were packed in the case in chronological order. In checking the serial numbers of the missing guns against the dates Ford had them engraved, Hannegan figured out he had started with the gun in the top left corner of the case and worked straight across. And the gun unaccounted for is the seventh, not the first.'

I thought this over dubiously, then asked, 'Hannegan talk to this jeweler personally?'

'Just over the phone. He intended to follow it up with a visit.'

'I'll save him a trip by making that check myself,' I said. 'I'll let you know what I get. Find anything else of interest in Ford's apartment?'

Day grinned sourly. 'Not bearing on his murder. They found a few dirty pictures.'

I raised my brows. 'Oh? Got them here?'

'You reached the stage where you like to look at dirty pictures?' the inspector demanded.

'According to Ford's wife, he used them for blackmail,' I said patiently. 'Blackmail makes a lovely motive for murder.'

For a moment he scowled at me, then pulled open his top drawer, took out a large manila envelope, withdrew a number of glossy five-by-eight prints and tossed them to me.

There were eleven pictures altogether, and all the poses were approximately the same. A man sat on the edge of a bed, his back to the camera so that his face was invisible, and a woman lay in his arms, her back across his knees. In addition to the pose, all had three other things in common. Despite only his back being visible, the same man was identifiable in each picture; the bed and room were the same; and in each case both the man and woman were naked.

The women were all different, however. The camera angle was such that, although the man's face could not be seen, his companion's face in each picture was clearly visible.

'You mean to tell me you didn't even suspect these were blackmail pictures?' I inquired.

'I assumed they were just standard pornography Ford had bought under the counter somewhere to gloat over in private,' Day said. 'That man in the pictures isn't Ford. Too broad through the shoulders.'

'Ford's confederate,' I told him. 'I'd guess these were infrared pictures. It's not a new gag. In the dark, the guy in the picture from some concealed spot. She wouldn't even know a snap had been taken until either Ford or his confederate offered to sell it to her a few days later.'

The first time I had shuffled through the photographs, I had done it rapidly, barely glancing at each one. Now I went through a second time in a more leisurely manner. Halfway through, I stopped and whistled.

'What's the matter?' Day asked.

I began to suspect that I had done the inspector an injustice, and he actually hadn't as yet given the pictures a close inspection. For if he had, I am sure he would have recognized the face which caused my whistle as quickly as I did.

I tossed the glossy print over to him.

He studied it with gradually widening eyes. There, lying in the broad-shouldered man's arms and smiling up at him lazily, was Bubbles Duval.

17

It took a bit of argument to talk Warren Day into letting me borrow the picture of Bubbles and the broad-shouldered man. The inspector was all for dragging the girl down to headquarters and sweating out of her the name of Ford's confederate.

I finally convinced him that since I knew the girl personally, and she seemed to have some liking for me, I could probably get more out of her than some strange cop.

The only other information I got from Warren Day was that Thomas Henry's bond hearing at nine o'clock that morning had come to nothing. Despite the legal efforts of the expensive Harvey Brighton, the judge had refused to allow bond, declaring that the nature of the alleged crime indicated that the accused, if guilty, was too inclined to violence for the court to assume responsibility for loosing him on society even temporarily until a jury had decided whether or not he was to be released permanently.

When I left headquarters, I drove over to West Lucas and dropped by Jessup's Jewelry Store. A gracious brunette with all the suavity of an undertaker's assistant came forward to wait on me.

When I asked to speak to the proprietor, she wanted to know what about. I told her about some gold engraving and she looked politely interested, but when I failed to elaborate, she smiled pleasantly and led me toward the rear of the store with the air of a headwaiter showing me to a table.

Mr. Jessup, whose first name was Samuel according to the discreet gold lettering on the front window I had noted on the way in, was closeted in a tiny workroom containing nothing but a table, a chair, and a rack of intricate tools. The tabletop was littered with rings, watches and other types of jewelry in various stages of repair, and at the moment the jeweler was resetting a stone in a rhinestone bracelet.

In contrast to his sophisticated clerk,

Samuel Jessup was as homey as red suspenders. He was a plump man of about fifty with a benign face and an air of extreme patience. When the brunette announced in a soft voice that he had a visitor, he nodded without looking up, and continued to work on the bracelet with a thin-nosed pair of pliers.

I waited quietly until he had made the last delicate adjustment, laid down the pliers and removed the powerful jeweler's glasses from his eyes. For them he substituted a plain horn-rimmed pair, then blinked up at me inquiringly.

Handing him my license, I waited until he had studied it, then said, 'I'm working with the Homicide Department on the Ford case. I have Inspector Day's permission to ask questions in the name of the department, and I'd like to ask you some. Maybe you'd like to check me by phone with Inspector Day first.'

He gave me a pleasant smile as he handed back my license. 'I don't think that will be necessary, Mr. Moon. I'm sure the help I'll be able to give you will be so small it won't matter whether you have police authority or not. As a matter of fact, I told some lieutenant everything I knew about Walter Ford over the phone.'

'That was Lieutenant Hannegan,' I said. 'Mind going over again what you told him?'

Jessup said he didn't mind at all. He still had the slip of paper on his desk containing the notes he had made from his files for Hannegan's benefit, and he referred to it to refresh his memory as he talked.

'The only work we've ever done for Mr. Ford was the engraving of gold initials on the ivory grips of six twenty-five-caliber automatic pistols,' he said. 'They all came in at different times, the first on March twelfth. It was picked up three days later. That was engraved M.S.'

'Madeline Strong,' I said.

'I wouldn't know what any of the initials stand for. The next came in May second, was picked up on the fourth, and the initials were H.D. Then on May fifteenth we engraved one A.M.'

Apparently those were the two women the police had located through Ford's address book and cleared as having no possible connection with the crime.

'Then we didn't do any more until last month,' Jessup went on. 'June eighth we engraved one E.K. and on June twenty-eighth B.D.'

Evelyn Karnes and Beatrice Duval, I thought, which jibed with the dates both girls claimed to have received their pistols from Ford.

'How about the last one?' I asked.

'That came in just a few days before Mr. Ford was killed. July seventh, to be exact. Our instructions were to engrave it T.H.'

'Did Ford bring all these guns in personally?'

'No. He sent them by Pickup Service and had them picked up the same way.' Then he frowned thoughtfully. 'At least, the last one came that way. I'd have to check with Leona about the others.'

When I looked at him without understanding, he explained, 'Usually I don't get out front much except when we're rushed, and we're hardly ever rushed. Leona handles the store trade and I work back here. Last week she was out sick and I had to handle everything, which is why this mess of work accumulated.' He gestured at the littered tabletop. 'So I know Pickup Service brought in the last gun, but Leona would have received all the others.'

Rising, he walked to the workroom door, saw that the suave brunette had no customers, and called her to the back of the shop.

'Those pistols of Mr. Ford's the police phoned me about,' he said. 'How'd they usually come in?'

'Mr. Ford always brought them in personally, and picked them up again when they were finished.'

Jessup thanked her, and when she had gone away again he sat down in the lone chair and looked up at me uneasily. 'Does that mean anything, Mr. Moon? The messenger brought along a note from Ford requesting a hurry-up job and asking us to have the gun ready the next day. I recall it was the same messenger boy who came after it.'

I frowned thoughtfully. 'This boy have

anything to identify himself?'

He looked even more uneasy. 'I didn't inquire, Mr. Moon. He just said he was from Pickup Service and gave me a large envelope containing the gun and note. Of course, under ordinary circumstances I would require identification before releasing a customer's property to a messenger, but since the same boy who brought the gun in came after it too, I hardly thought it necessary.'

Asking if I could use his phone, I looked up the number of Pickup Service and got hold of the dispatcher. After explaining who I was and that I was working with the authorization of Warren Day, I asked him to check his records for July seventh and eighth to see if he had had any calls — either from a Mr. Walter Ford or anyone else — for trips to Jessup's.

After about a five-minute wait, the dispatcher informed me the company had made no such delivery or pickup for Walter Ford or anyone else.

When I hung up, Jessup was looking worried.

'It's the sort of thing anybody would be taken in by,' I reassured him. 'Nobody will hold you responsible. I'd guess whoever it was had the engraving done simply hired some kid to act the part of a Pickup messenger. Probably he was waiting right outside the store while the boy was inside both times. How was the engraving paid for?'

'By the messenger, in cash.'

'It all fits,' I said. 'The person who ordered the engraving couldn't afford to let you see him because he wasn't Walter Ford, and he had to assume the police would make at least a routine check with you eventually. You've been a big help, Mr. Jessup.'

Asking if I could use his phone again, I dialed Warren Day's office. When I told the inspector what I had learned, he was silent for a moment.

Then he said, 'We've got to get hold of that kid and find out who hired him.'

'How?' I asked. 'There are probably ten thousand kids in town answering to the same description.'

'How about running a personal ad

offering a reward if he'll contact us? You know, 'If the young man who delivered a package to Jessup's Jewelry Store on July seventh and picked it up on July eighth will phone number so-and-so, it will be to his financial advantage.' Something on that order.'

'And have the murderer read it too? We'd find the kid all right. Dead.'

'Yeah,' he said in a dissatisfied voice. 'I guess we better just put out a general call. Let me talk to Jessup.'

When I relinquished the phone, apparently Day asked Jessup for a complete description of the messenger, for the jeweler said, 'About seventeen, Inspector. Five-ten, I'd say, and about a hundred and thirty pounds. Brown hair in a crew cut and a kind of long face. What? I don't know. Just an ordinary complexion. Neither dark nor light. Just ordinary. I don't know what color eyes he had. Both days he wore brown cotton slacks and a plain yellow sport shirt with the tail outside his belt. No, nobody else saw him because my girl was out sick last week and I was here alone.'

When he hung up, I had the feeling that I was finally getting my teeth into the case. Day's reaction to the fake messenger boy indicated he was now convinced Tom Henry had been framed, and from here on out I could expect an all-out effort on the part of Homicide to catch the real murderer instead of merely an effort to consolidate its case against my client.

As this was the first definite progress I had made — except for vague suspicions that there was something phony about the evidence against Thomas Henry — it occurred to me that Madeline Strong would want to know about it at once. Since her apartment was less than a mile from Jessup's, I drove over instead of phoning.

Madeline's place was on Park Lane near Mason Avenue, one of the most expensive residential districts in town. Since the opposite side of Park Lane was Midland Park, the view from the apartment house was one of trees and well-kept grass as far as you could see. The view alone probably added fifty dollars a month to the rent, I thought, and wondered again just how much money the girl had.

Madeline's apartment was 3-C. A virtually silent self-service elevator took me to the third floor, and I waded along an ankle-deep carpet to the door of 3-C. There was no bell in evidence, but when I lifted a highly polished brass knocker in the shape of a knight's shield, it caused a mellow tinkle of chimes within the apartment. When I released the knocker, it sank silently back into place instead of clattering against its metal faceplate.

Barney Amhurst came to the door. When he saw me, his dimples showed in a smile of pleasure.

'Come in, Mr. Moon,' he said hospitably. 'Madeline and I were just talking about you.'

I followed him through a large living room furnished with quiet but expensive taste, through an equally tastefully furnished dining room, and into a bright and immaculate kitchen. Madeline Strong was in the act of making a plate of chicken-salad sandwiches.

When Amhurst entered the room, she looked up at him inquiringly, then saw me. Dropping the spoon she was using to ladle mayonnaise, she came toward me with both hands outstretched.

'I was just thinking about calling you, Mr. Moon. Have you learned anything new?'

'A little,' I said, letting her work off emotion by squeezing both my hands. The emotion was for Tom Henry, I knew, and was transferred to me only because she hoped I could give her some news about her fiancé, but it was pleasant to be on the receiving end of even secondhand affection from such a pretty girl.

I glanced at the plate of sandwiches, then at a wall clock which said eleven forty-five. 'I didn't mean to barge in on you at lunchtime. It didn't occur to me you'd eat this early.'

'We had an early breakfast because we had to be in court by nine.' Releasing my hands, she glanced at Amhurst and said — with a touch of self-consciousness, as though she felt called upon to explain his presence — 'Barney was good enough to drive me down, so I invited him for lunch. Will you stay too? I only have sandwiches and cake, but there's plenty of both.'

As there seemed to be enough sand-wiches on the plate to feed an average wedding party, I said, 'Thanks. Be glad to. I can bring you up to date during lunch.'

18

We had lunch in the dining room, Barney and I volunteering to set the table while Madeline made coffee. As we munched on chicken-salad sandwiches, Madeline repeated what Warren Day had already told me about the judge refusing to release Tom Henry on bond.

'I think we've finally got Homicide on our side,' I said. 'He hasn't exactly come right out and said it, but I believe Warren Day is as convinced as you are that Tom Henry was framed.'

When I told her about my visit to Jessup's and the resulting pickup call that had gone out for the pseudo messenger, she almost went into ecstasies.

'Now they'll have to let Tom out,' she said. 'They haven't a thing to hold him on.'

'I'm afraid it isn't that simple,' I deflated her. 'From the police point of view, there's still the possibility that it was

Henry himself who stole the gun from Ford's set and had it initialed. If you asked them, they'd probably admit they couldn't think of any plausible reason for his doing such a thing, but I'm sure they won't release him until they definitely establish who did have the engraving done.'

This subdued her jubilation, but she was too happy at the possibility of Tom being cleared to remain depressed very long. A moment later she was inquiring eagerly, 'How long will it take to locate this messenger boy? Do you think they might find him today?'

'They have only a rather slim description,' I hedged. 'And the kid may not live anywhere near Jessup's. Whoever hired him to pose as a Pickup messenger may have brought him from clear across town, or even from out of town.'

'Oh,' she said, depressed again.

'Day wanted to run a box ad offering a reward to the boy for coming forward with information,' I said. 'Probably the kid doesn't realize he was involved in anything illegal and wouldn't hesitate to report in if he saw the ad. But there's always the possibility the murderer would see the ad too, and decide the kid was too dangerous to leave alive. We have to try to locate him quietly.'

'Do you think Ed Friday is behind this?' Barney asked abruptly.

I raised an eyebrow at him. 'Why do you ask?'

He looked slightly embarrassed. 'Well, it was pretty obvious he was sore at Walt the other night for passing at Evelyn. And I think that boy Max of his would kill anyone Friday told him to. Then Madeline told me you asked her if she knew of any reason Friday wouldn't want you to look into the case, which leads me to assume he must have approached you in an attempt to get you to drop it.'

Ignoring the implied question in his final sentence, I said, 'I've been considering Friday as a possibility, but somehow I can't see him risking murder over a woman. I'd be happier if I could discover some other motive for him to get rid of Ford. Of course, there's always the possibility Friday was one of Ford's 'blackmail victims.'

'Blackmail?' Amhurst repeated, open-mouthed.

'Ford had a habit of snapping infrared photographs of women. He had a confederate whose job was to get the women into compromising positions. There isn't any evidence that his blackmailing activities took any form other than that, but blackmailers aren't very particular. I suspect Ford would have put the screws to anyone he had something on, and I understand he once worked for Friday. Possibly he was holding something out of the past over Friday's head, and Friday got tired of paying off.'

'I don't think so,' Madeline objected. 'They always seemed friendly enough until Walt started paying too much attention to Evelyn. Mr. Friday always seemed to me to treat Walt with a touch of tolerant contempt, but I think he liked him all right. At least, I never noticed anything in his manner to suggest he feared Walt.'

'Wasn't it Ford who brought Friday into the Huntsafe Company?' I asked.

'Yeah,' Amhurst said. 'That was part of my deal with Walt. I agreed to give him a share of the stock if he could get legislative action on the Gimmick and also produce a backer for manufacture.'

'I know,' I said. 'A ten percent share, according to Ford's widow. That right?'

Barney flushed slightly. 'That's right. Ten percent.'

I examined his flush curiously. 'Wasn't that kind of high payment for the services involved?'

Madeline said to Amhurst, 'You ought to look embarrassed, Barney.' To me, she said, 'The only inventor I ever knew who had any business sense was my brother. He always had an ironbound contract for everything he did, and it was always in his own favor. But Barney hasn't any more business sense than my Tom. He'd have given all the stock away if I hadn't found out what he was doing and put a stop to it. He signed over twenty percent to me to cover Lloyd's interest in the invention, though he wasn't legally required to give me anything; ten percent to Walt Ford; and forty percent to Ed Friday for putting

188

up the money for manufacture. He's only retained a thirty percent interest for himself. If I had known what he was doing in time, I would have stopped it. We didn't need Mr. Friday's money. I would have backed the company myself for another twenty percent interest, and Barney could have retained sixty percent. And there was no necessity for giving Walt Ford *any* interest. He simply should have been on the payroll as an employee of the company.'

Barney said defensively, 'At the time I made the agreement, I didn't have anything to offer but a share of the invention.'

They were still arguing the point amiably when we finished lunch. Madeline refused our offer to help with the dishes, saying she merely wanted to stack them, as she intended to run right over to the jail and tell Tom the good news and didn't want to take the time to do dishes.

The rest of that afternoon I spent catching up on the sleep I had missed the night before. Late in the afternoon, I phoned Warren Day to check if any progress had been made in tracking down

Alberto Thomaso. The inspector told me the address shown on the youthful gunman's driving license had been correct, but by the time the police checked it, the bird had flown.

1812 Sixth Street was a rooming house, Day said, and according to the landlady, Alberto had come home some time in the wee hours, packed and had taken off immediately. The landlady's room was just below Thomaso's and apparently she was a light sleeper, for she had heard him come in and leave again. She hadn't turned on a light to see the time, but estimated this had occurred around four a.m.

'We found the Chrysler abandoned near Midland Park,' the inspector said. 'The owner didn't even know it was stolen until we gave him a ring. Seems he's been on a toot the last few days and thought he just couldn't remember where he parked it. We also ran down the owner of that river cottage.'

'Get anything from him?'

'Nothing important. He's a guy named Robert Baxter. Thomaso rented the cottage from him last summer, but it hasn't had a tenant this summer. Apparently Thomaso just decided to appropriate it for a couple of weeks, because Baxter claims he didn't have authorization from him to use it.'

'Get anything on the Woodsman?'

Day's voice turned pleased. 'Yeah. Ballistics tied it to an unsolved gang killing of nearly a year ago. This kid is even dumber than most hoods. Imagine a guy dumb enough to hang onto a gun after he's used it for murder.'

'I can't,' I said. 'Even Alberto isn't that dumb. I hate to spoil your dreams, but I'll bet my little playmate is clear of that one. Five gets you ten he bought it in a pawnshop subsequent to your year-old murder.'

'I suppose,' Day said glumly. 'I thought of that too. If a ready-made solution to a killing ever fell in my lap, I wouldn't believe it.'

'Making any progress in locating that kid messenger?'

'Naw. It's like looking for a needle in a haystack. Hannegan came up with a bright idea we're going to try in the morning. On the off-chance that the kid may be enrolled in summer school, we're asking all the high schools to question all male students fitting the description. Not one kid in ten goes to summer school, but it's a chance.'

I told the inspector I'd check with him again the next day, and rang off.

Since my date with Fausta was at nine and I wanted to see Bubbles Duval first, I showered and dressed before dinner. At seven I was at Bubbles' apartment and was waiting in front of her door when she came in from work.

'Manny!' she squealed enthusiastically when she saw me. 'We going out again tonight?'

'No,' I said. 'I just want to talk with you a few minutes.'

Looking mildly disappointed, she handed me her key. As I slipped it into the lock, she managed to stand so close our shoulders brushed, making it difficult for me to manipulate the key.

When, after a bit of fumbling because of the crowded work quarters, I managed to get the door open, she squeezed past in such a manner that her breasts momentarily rubbed across my biceps. Inside, she tossed her purse onto a chair, seated herself in the center of the sofa, and patted the place next to her.

Shaking my head, I came to a stop directly before her and stood looking down at her.

'I'm going to show you something, Bubbles, and I'm afraid it's going to upset you a little.'

Taking the photograph of Bubbles and the broad-shouldered man from my pocket, I held it in front of her.

Her eyes grew wide and slowly her face turned crimson. 'Where did you get that?' she yelled, making a wild grab for it.

Jerking it out of her reach, I put the picture back in my pocket. 'Sorry, Bubbles. If it was mine, I'd let you tear it up, but it's police evidence and I have to return it.'

'What do you want?' she asked finally.

'I want to know about this picture.'

'Isn't it self-evident? Walter Ford took it. You must know that. It's one of the pictures you were talking about last night.

Only this one was supposed to be destroyed. I watched Walter burn it myself.'

'You can make an unlimited number of prints from a negative,' I said dryly. 'How about telling me the whole story? I'll guarantee there won't be any publicity. The cops do everything possible to protect the reputations of blackmail victims. If you're ever called to testify against this guy in the picture, you'll appear in the public records as Jane Doe. And you may never even be called. The cops have a whole series of similar pictures involving other women which they may decide to use instead of yours.'

'They couldn't use me,' Bubbles said. 'I wasn't a blackmail victim.'

19

I blinked at her. 'How was that again?'

'It was all a mistake,' Bubbles said. 'I thought he was rich and he thought I was rich. When they found out I was just a working girl, they dropped the blackmail attempt.'

I decided to unscramble this array of personal pronouns one at a time. 'Who did you think was rich? Walter Ford?'

She shook her head.

'Daniel Cumberland. He's the man in the picture.'

'And when you say 'they' dropped the blackmail attempt, do you mean Ford and this Cumberland?'

'Yes.'

'Let's start over at the beginning,' I suggested. 'Just tell me the whole story.'

So she started at the beginning and told me the whole story.

Daniel Cumberland was an extremely good-looking man of about thirty, Bubbles told me. He was also extremely well-dressed and managed to exude the affluent air of a successful businessman. His front was posing as junior vice-president of one of the local manufacturing plants.

Bubbles met him casually at the bar of one of the more exclusive cocktail lounges, and in a misguided attempt to impress him had colored her own background as fantastically as Cumberland was coloring his. She let him know that she was executive manager of Saxon and Harder's, where her father was president of the board of directors.

Properly impressed, Cumberland went all out in pursuit of Bubbles. From the cocktail lounge he took her to dinner, then to a show, and afterward suggested they have a drink at his apartment. Bubbles admitted she was as charmed by Cumberland as he seemed to be by her; and, not possessing any great degree of maidenly restraint, she welcomed the suggestion with enthusiasm.

This eventually led to the results indicated in the photograph.

It was two nights later that Walter Ford

dropped by her apartment, showed her the photograph and offered to sell it to her for a thousand dollars.

At first she was enraged, Bubbles said, and threatened to call the police. Ford, apparently an old hand in such dealings, merely told her to go ahead. He would simply walk out the moment she picked up the phone, he told her, and she could report her head off. Since up to that time he hadn't told her his name and she hadn't the faintest idea who he was, Bubbles realized she might have some difficulty making her complaint stick. When Ford also assured her a copy of the photograph would be mailed to every member of the board of directors at Saxon and Harder's the next day unless she came to terms, she further realized she probably would lose her job unless she talked him out of this action.

So, quite calmly, she told him she was merely a dress model instead of executive manager of Saxon and Harder's, had less than a hundred dollars in the bank, and couldn't afford to pay him a nickel.

Once he became convinced she was

telling the truth, Ford's first reaction was anger at having wasted his time. Then the humor of the situation struck him and he suddenly seemed to decide it was outrageously funny.

Why, after such an introduction, Bubbles didn't kick the man out of her apartment and refuse to have anything more to do with him, I will never understand. But after Ford ceremoniously burned the photograph in an ashtray, she actually forgave him. The only explanation I can think of is that the girl's moral and ethical standards must have been as flexible as the blackmailers', because she didn't even seem to harbor resentment over the use Cumberland and Ford had attempted to make of her. She seemed more resentful over the discovery that Ford had retained another copy of the picture than she did over the attempted blackmail.

'I don't know,' I said with frustration. 'I guess you and I must have gone to different Sunday schools. Did you also continue to date this Cumberland fellow?'

'Oh, no. Not him.'

I was contemplating that at least she

had saved me the mental effort of trying to understand her motives on that score when she burst the bubble by adding, 'I phoned him once, but I guess he lost interest in me when Walter told him I didn't have any money.'

At that point I gave up trying to understand her at all. 'Where did this Daniel Cumberland live?'

'He has an apartment at Lincoln and Nebraska. It's listed in the book.'

Checking her phone book, I discovered that, sure enough, a Daniel Cumberland was listed at 428 Lincoln Avenue. Dialing the operator, I asked if that phone was still listed under Cumberland's name.

It was.

Well, well, I thought, the bird hadn't even flown. And since it was now only a little after seven-thirty, I decided to look up Walter Ford's blackmail partner before keeping my date with Fausta.

428 Lincoln Avenue was a three-story apartment house in an upper-middle-class neighborhood. Two walls of the small foyer were lined with mail slots, and by checking the cards beneath them I learned that

Daniel Cumberland occupied apartment 1-B. The mail boxes had glass fronts, and I noted there was quite an accumulation of mail in Cumberland's.

No one answered the door apartment 1-B.

Returning to the foyer, I discovered 1-A was listed as the manager's apartment. When I rang that bell, an elderly man with curling snow-white hair and an equally snow-white mustache came to the door. He admitted he was the apartment-house manager, and said his name was Stanley Bush.

'I'm Manville Moon,' I said, showing him my license. 'I'm working with the police on a case in which one of your tenants is an important witness. He doesn't seem to be home, and I'd like to take a look at his apartment. I haven't a search warrant, but I can get one if I have to. It would be simpler all around if you'd let me take a quick look now, though. With you present, of course.'

He chewed thoughtfully at his mustache. 'Which tenant?'

I indicated the door across the hall

from his own. 'Cumberland.'

'Hmm. Say you're working with the police?'

'Under Inspector Warren Day of Homicide. I can give you his home phone number if you'd like to check me.'

He gave me a careful looking-over. 'Don't think that will be necessary, young fellow. Look honest enough to me. Besides, I'll be right next to you to make sure you don't lift nothing.'

He disappeared for a moment, returning with a ring of keys. Selecting one, he opened the door of apartment 1-B. The odor hit us the moment the door was open, and we both knew what it was at once. It was not strong, but it was unmistakably the odor of decaying flesh.

'Oh-oh,' Stanley Bush said, pushing the door shut again as soon as we were inside. 'Thought it funny I hadn't seen Cumberland around for a couple of days.'

The apartment was expensively furnished, but at the moment it was a mess. Every drawer in the front room had been pulled out and dumped on the floor, books had been pulled from their shelves, and even sofa and chair cushions were strewed around the room. Through an open door we could see a similar cyclone had hit the bedroom.

'Somebody's been looking mighty hard for something,' old Bush remarked.

He sniffed at the penetrating odor, then followed his nose through the apartment into the kitchen. There we found Walter Ford's partner in blackmail.

Daniel Cumberland may have been as handsome as Bubbles said when he was alive, but he made an exceedingly ugly corpse. Largely this was because of the temperature, for all the windows were closed.

The man lay on his back on the kitchen floor, a bullet hole between his eyes and a pool of dried blood circling his head. He was dressed in pajamas, robe and slippers; a half-empty cup of coffee sat on the table in front of the chair in which he had apparently been sitting when he was shot. I noted that another cup and saucer, washed clean, rested on the sink drainboard.

From all appearances, the man had

been drinking coffee with someone he knew well enough to serve in the kitchen when he was killed. And from his attire, his guest must have been a late and unexpected caller. Apparently, after murdering his host, the killer had carefully washed out his own coffee cup, then searched the apartment from one end to the other. He had not even missed the kitchen, for it was as much of a shambles as the rest of the rooms.

Cumberland had been dead well over twenty-four hours, I guessed. Possibly even forty-eight, for the body was already bloated.

The elderly apartment manager said, 'Let's get some of this stink out,' and started towards the kitchen windows.

'Hold it,' I advised. 'We don't touch a thing before the cops get here.'

Stopping, he scratched his head. 'What now, then?'

'Now we lock this place up again, go back to your apartment and phone the police.'

'Suits me,' he said. 'I've seen everything I want to see here.'

20

A Sergeant John Kietel, of the night Homicide detail, showed up in answer to my phone call. In addition to the usual retinue of scientific assistants, he brought with him another detective whom he didn't bother to introduce, but whose first name I gathered was Harry.

Harry was of the Hannegan school. He didn't open his mouth once during the whole investigation, merely nodding agreeably whenever the sergeant gave him an order, then meticulously carrying out instructions.

I explained to Sergeant Kietel how Cumberland tied in with the Walter Ford case, and how I happened to have called on the dead man.

I stayed around long enough to get the preliminary reports. The medical examiner guessed Cumberland had been dead thirty to forty-eight hours, adding he might be able to reduce the span after an autopsy. Since Walter Ford's murder had taken place only a little less than forty-eight hours before, it seemed likely to me that the two killings had taken place the same night.

Possibly the killer had gone straight from polishing off one victim to murder the other.

No weapon was found in the apartment; nor any fingerprints, aside from the dead man's, clear enough to be useable for comparison purposes.

The apartment consisted of four rooms and a bath. The front room, kitchen, bedroom and bath had been searched thoroughly by the killer, as evidenced by the mess left behind, but in the dining room the drawers of the sideboard were untouched. The logical conclusion was that either something had frightened the killer into stopping his search, or he had found what he was looking for in the dining room. When the painstaking Harry found a section of baseboard which slid upward to disclose a small secret compartment, we decided the latter was the case.

The compartment was empty.

By then, it was nearly nine, and I broke away to keep my date with Fausta. Sergeant Kietel, still awed by my supposed influence with his chief, didn't even give me the customary instruction to stay available as a witness.

Mouldy Greene looked at me in surprise when I walked into El Patio.

'What's the matter, Sarge?' he asked. 'You and Fausta get your wires crossed?'

'Not that I know of. Why?'

'She said she was going over to your place when she left here a half-hour ago.'

'That's funny,' I said, puzzled. 'She knew I was picking her up here at nine.'

Mouldy lifted his massive shoulders in a shrug. Then a customer at one of the tables in the cocktail lounge called him over to introduce him to a friend, and while he was occupied I went on back to Fausta's office. I used her private phone to dial my own number, and Fausta answered at once.

'What's up?' I inquired. 'What the devil are you doing there?'

'Waiting for you, my one. Where are you?'

'Where I'm supposed to be,' I told her. 'At El Patio. Didn't you say pick you up here?'

'And did you not phone a message to my headwaiter saying you were hung up and I was to take a taxi to your apartment?' she countered.

'No,' I said slowly. 'But if someone did, I don't like the smell of it. Anyone else there?'

'I am all alone. Did you not leave that note on the door saying the door was unlocked and I was to wait inside?'

'Cripes, no,' I said with rising panic. 'Listen, Fausta. Go lock both the front and back doors right now. Then sit there and don't let anyone in until I get there. Got that?'

There was a sudden gasp, a half-articulate cry of pain, and then silence.

'Fausta!' I shouted.

'She decided to take a little nap, friend,' a low voice said in my ear. 'But don't worry about her. I'm as good with a sap as I am with a twenty-two. The bump won't even show.'

The voice was that of the young

gunman, Alberto Thomaso.

Forcing my voice to come out deadly calm, I asked, 'What do you want, Al?'

'Me? Nothing, friend. I just work here. My boss wants a thing or two, though.'

'Who's your boss?'

He let out a cynical chuckle. 'Let's not waste time with silly questions, pal. Where are you?'

'At El Patio.'

'Where at El Patio?'

'In Fausta's private office.'

'Alone?'

'Yes.'

'What's the number of that phone?'

In a tight voice I read it off from the center plate.

'I'll call you back in about an hour,' Alberto said. 'You answer personally. If anyone else answers, your blonde girl-friend is done. Got it?'

'I've got it,' I said bleakly.

'Another thing. Every five minutes until I call, somebody else will ring that number. If the line is busy, the girl is cooked. That's to make sure you don't make any outside calls.'

When I made no answer, he said, 'Neat, ain't it? The boss figured when you got Miss Moreni's message that you'd use her office to phone here, and you'd be there all alone. You're stuck. If you get far enough from that phone so you can't answer it instantly when it rings, or if you use it to call the cops, the girl gets it. On the other hand, if you play along, I guarantee she won't get hurt.'

'I'll play along,' I said. 'But I've got some instructions too.'

He emitted a little laugh. 'You ain't in much of a position to give instructions.'

'No,' I admitted, 'but I'm giving them anyway. Don't hurt Fausta and I'll do whatever you say. If anything happens to her, I'll hunt you down and kill you. That's a guarantee too.'

'Nothing's going to happen to her,' he assured me. 'That is, nothing but being locked up for a time. You'll hear from me in an hour.'

The phone went dead.

While I was talking to Alberto, my mind had been too full of concern for Fausta to even wonder why she was being kidnaped. But the moment he hung up, I began to understand the reason. And the more I thought about it, the more amazed I became at the mixture of cleverness and stupidity behind the kidnaping.

It seemed obvious to me that Walter Ford's killer had engineered the snatch, hoping to use Fausta as a lever to force me to abandon my investigation of the case. The manner in which Fausta was kidnaped had been clever enough, but the motive struck me as almost incredibly stupid. For even if it accomplished its purpose of making me drop the investigation, the killer should have known that eventually I would tell the whole story to the police, and to them it would simply constitute further evidence that someone was desperately trying to prevent the frame of Thomas Henry from coming to light.

All through the case it was impressing me more and more that Ford's killer possessed an amazing mixture of brilliance and stark stupidity. These thoughts skipped through my mind almost instantaneously, then my whole attention reverted to plans for getting Fausta out of her situation. The elaborate plot for making sure I would stick close to the phone and couldn't call the police, like most of the killer's plots, had a cardinal defect. I had phoned my apartment from Fausta's private phone, which had a direct line into the building. Next to it on her desk was a phone which went through El Patio's switchboard.

The inspector dislikes being disturbed on police business after five o'clock in the evening, but at the moment I wasn't concerned about anyone's feelings. I cut him off in the middle of a growl.

'Listen fast, Inspector,' I said. 'That young hood Alberto Thomaso has put the snatch on Fausta. Why, doesn't matter right now, but I just talked to him on the phone. I'm in Fausta's office and he had Fausta at my apartment.'

When he interrupted to ask how this arrangement came about, I said, 'Just hold the questions and listen, Inspector. My instructions are to wait right here, where Alberto will phone again in an hour. Meantime, a confederate of Alberto's will call me every five minutes on Fausta's phone to make sure I'm still here and I'm not calling the police. If I don't answer, or if the line is busy, Fausta gets it. Alberto doesn't know Fausta has two phones. I'm calling on the second.'

At that moment Fausta's private phone pealed.

'There's the call now,' I said. 'Hold it and don't make any squawking noises, or the caller might realize I've got a second phone.'

Laying down the one phone, I picked up the other and said, 'Moon speaking.'

There was silence, a click and a buzzing noise. I replaced the receiver and picked up the other again.

'Here's what I want,' I said rapidly. 'First, get some cops to my flat. Probably they'll get there too late, but it's a slim chance. Next, get somebody here fast. Fausta has extensions to both phones in her apartment upstairs. A cop upstairs can listen in on the extension of her private phone, and use the switchboard phone to arrange for tracing the calls. Got it?'

'I can arrange for the last from here,' the inspector said. 'What's that private phone number?'

When I read it to him, he said, 'Check. I won't call you back because the phone might ring just as you were talking to your caller on the other phone. Think I'll come out there soon as I get things moving.'

He rang off.

During the next twenty minutes, Fausta's phone rang on schedule every five minutes, and each time I answered I was greeted only by silence, the click of the other phone hanging up, and then the buzz of the dial tone. At the end of twenty minutes, Warren Day walked in.

Giving me a gruff nod, he asked which was the phone connecting with the club's switchboard, and, when I pointed to it, picked it up. In a crisp tone he informed the operator he was Inspector Warren Day of Homicide, told her to get him police headquarters, and instructed her to leave the connection open until she was told to close it.

A moment later the inspector was

saying, 'Blake? Any news from Moon's flat?'

After listening a moment and giving a noncommittal grunt, Day said, 'I'm having this line kept open so I'll be in constant communication with you. Put a man on it and keep him there with the receiver to his ear so all I'll have to do is pick up the phone if I have any orders. If you want me, have your man let out a whistle. I'll be close enough to the phone to hear it.'

The phone crackled as Blake indicated he understood instructions. With a final grunt the inspector laid the receiver on the desk.

'We can't have this thing ringing,' he said to me in explanation. 'It might sound off in the middle of one of those five-minute checks.'

'What was the report from my place?' I asked.

'Negative. Nobody there. No sign of violence. What do you make of this, Moon? Alberto gone nuts?'

The private phone rang before I could answer. When I had listened to the usual silence and hung up again, I said, 'Walter

Ford's killer has, apparently. Alberto is just stooging for him. Or her, as the case may be.'

Day looked puzzled. 'What's this snatch supposed to accomplish?'

'Get me off the case, I suppose. At least, my guess is that the ransom will be for me to drop the thing. Maybe I'll have to agree to take a long trip.'

The phone Day had laid on the desk emitted a shrill whistle. The inspector picked it up, barked, 'Yeah?' and then listened intently.

'Good,' he said finally. 'Let me know as soon as they report in.' He laid the phone down again.

When I looked at him questioningly, he said, 'The phone company has a supervisor tracing every call that comes to Fausta's private line. That last checkup call you got came from a four-party residential phone. There's no way to check which party, but there's a squad car on the way to each address right now.'

It seemed to me it was about time for another checkup call. I glanced at my watch, then uneasily looked at it again.

'It's eight minutes since the last call,' I said. 'Maybe our killer got cagey.'

Apparently he had, for there were no more calls until Alberto himself finally phoned. After some discussion, the inspector and I decided Alberto's confederate probably never intended to continue phoning at five-minute intervals for the full hour. The device was designed to give Alberto time to get Fausta well away from the vicinity of my flat, we reasoned; and after the confederate made several calls, the risk of my using the phone to call the police was less than the risk of his calls being traced.

Another whistle from the phone connected to headquarters caused Day to pick it up again. When he had listened, then acknowledged the report with his usual grunt, he looked at me with a curious expression on his face.

'What now?' I asked.

'This one is a dilly. Three of the addresses on that four-party line turned out to be families who never heard of either you or Fausta. The last one was Thomas Henry's basement flat.'

21

'Thomas Henry?' I repeated incredulously. 'But he's in jail!'

'Yeah,' the inspector said. 'And his place is locked up tight. No evidence even that anyone had been there. But that's where the calls must have come from. Somebody walked in, made all those calls, then left and locked the door behind him. Maybe we better ask young Henry who might have a key to his flat.'

I shook my head hopelessly. 'I checked the back entrance to his place. It has one of those old-fashioned locks any dime-store skeleton key will open.'

We had to wait nearly another full half-hour after that before the call finally came from Alberto. I spent it walking up and down, clenching and unclenching my hands. Day spent it slouched in a chair, chewing on an unlighted and increasingly tattered cigar butt, and following my pacing with his eyes.

Belatedly, it occurred to me that Day knew nothing of the murder of Daniel Cumberland, as the report wouldn't reach his desk until morning. Grasping the chance to wrench my mind from Fausta's plight, I brought him up to date on my visit with Bubbles and my later discovery of Cumberland's body.

'This killer really is panicky,' he remarked. 'Two murders and two kidnapings. You think maybe this Bubbles dame could be behind all this?'

Wearily, I ran my hands through my hair. 'I don't know. Conceivably, she could have hired Alberto to kill both Ford and Cumberland. There's the motive of the blackmail picture; except that if the story Bubbles told me is true, it isn't much of a motive. I like Ed Friday as a suspect better. Only the panic this killer is in doesn't seem to fit Friday.'

'It occur to you Alberto may be working on his own?' Day asked. 'Maybe the Ford-Cumberland team was blackmailing him for something.'

I shook my head. 'He isn't smart enough to have engineered the frame against Henry. His whole record shows he's nothing but a two-bit punk. He's just a hired hand.'

The inspector said musingly, 'As soon as we get Fausta out of this jam, I think I'll go over Ed Friday a little.'

It was ten minutes beyond the single hour Alberto had said I would have to wait when the phone finally rang. Though I had been awaiting it with growing impatience, the sudden peal of the bell nearly made me jump out of my skin.

Picking up the phone, I said harshly, 'Moon speaking.'

'Hi, friend,' Alberto's low voice said. 'I see you've been a good boy and stuck right by the phone. I just talked to my boss, who tells me you behaved nice about not tying the phone up by making any outside calls too. You all alone?'

'I followed your instructions exactly,' I said in the same harsh tone. 'Is Fausta all right?'

'Except for a little headache. Now here's the shake, pal. Your girl stays right where she is, snug and cozy, for a full two weeks. You tell the people who work for her there that you and her are going on a little vacation. Then go up to her apartment, pack some of her stuff in a grip and take the grip to your own flat. Just leave it there.' He emitted a small chuckle. 'You can lock the door. I got a key that opens any lock. Then ... '

'Just a minute,' I interrupted. 'Suppose Fausta's staff suspect something? She isn't in the habit of running off on trips without advance notice.'

'That's your problem, friend. Just make sure it's a good story. Because at the first sign of cop curiosity, you can kiss your girl goodbye.'

'All right,' I said. 'I'll make the story good.'

'Now, after you get Miss Moreni's bag to your apartment, pack what you need for yourself and catch a plane for anywhere you want to go, so long as it's at least a thousand miles away. When you get there, send yourself a telegram to your own apartment giving your location and a phone number where you can be reached. I'll take care of collecting the telegram. After that, you just sit tight. At the end of two weeks I'll turn the dame loose, give her your out-of-town phone number, and she can call you and tell you to come home. By the time you get here, I'll be a thousand miles away, so don't bother to hunt for me. Got all that?'

I said, 'I think so, but it's pretty elaborate. Let me repeat it back to you.'

'No thanks, pal. You got it all right, and I don't like to talk too long. Goodbye now.'

'Wait a minute!' I said. 'I'm willing to co-operate a hundred percent because I don't want anything to happen to Fausta. But how do I know I can trust you? I want some kind of evidence she's all right.'

'Like me to send you one of her ears?' he asked savagely.

With an effort, I controlled my voice. 'I want an airmail special-delivery letter in her own handwriting as soon as I wire my address. There's no risk in that for you. I'll wait forty-eight hours after I send my wire. If a letter doesn't arrive by then, I'll be back in town on the next plane looking for your scalp. Tell that to your boss.'

'Sure, pal. I'll pass the word along. Meantime, you follow instructions. And remember, one peep to the cops, and the next time you see your blonde, she'll be on a marble slab.'

He hung up before I could get in another word.

I looked at Warren Day with desperation in my eyes. It was barely three minutes since the phone had rung.

'Why couldn't you hold him longer?' the inspector growled. Picking up the other phone, he said sharply, 'Did they get a trace on that call?'

After listening a moment, he said, 'Okay. We'll take the rest of it on my car's two-way. Tell Blake I want constant reports as they come in.'

He hung up the phone instead of laying it down again.

'They had Alberto pinpointed, and got his location on the air within forty-five seconds of the time he called. He phoned from a tavern over on the East Side. There was a squad car cruising only six blocks from there, and possibly they made it in time. We should know before we get there ourselves.'

We passed through the dining room and cocktail lounge so rapidly that customers turned to stare in our wake.

At the front door Mouldy Greene said in a surprised voice, 'You still here, Sarge? Thought you'd gone after Fausta long ago.'

We both brushed by without answering, which was a mistake. For when we reached Day's car at the bottom of El Patio's front steps, we found Mouldy right behind us. As Day and I crowded into the rear seat, Mouldy opened the front door and plumped himself next to the driver.

Turning sidewise, he scowled at me. 'It just registered on me that something's up,' he said. 'What's happened to Fausta?'

'Corner of Fifth and Martin,' Day snapped at the driver. 'Open it up, and keep the two-way on.'

The chauffeur seemed to realize that Day's mild 'Open it up' meant jet-speed. He took off like a rocket ship, his siren wild before we even reached the stone pillars at the entrance to the club's driveway. It was something like eight miles across the heaviest-trafficked part of town to Fifth and Martin, but I believe we made it in less than ten minutes.

Halfway across town, the radio reported that the police had arrived at the tavern just as Alberto came out, and that there had been some shooting. One of the two-man police team had been knocked out of action with a shoulder wound, Sergeant Blake's voice said from the radio, and the other cop had Alberto cornered in a flat above the tavern. Other police were on the way to the scene, he went on, but since the radio of the original car was now unmanned, there wouldn't be any additional reports until another squad car got there.

We arrived at Fifth and Martin before any further reports were forthcoming.

The tavern was a corner building, separated from the one next to it by only a four-foot areaway. As we arrived, the police were in the act of shoving back the gathering crowd and roping off the street. Searchlights bathed three sides of the building in a bright glare, and a fourth light was directed into the areaway so that any attempt by the cornered man to cross to the next building could be spotted immediately.

A uniformed cop with the gold badge of a lieutenant seemed to be directing the operation. Stepping to his side, Warren Day asked him to report the situation.

'Oh, hello, sir,' the lieutenant said respectfully. 'I'm not sure myself what the situation is, except we've got somebody trapped in that upstairs flat. All I know is I got a radio report of a shooting, and when I got here I found Officer Healey had been wounded and his partner, Thompkins, had the gunman cornered. I haven't had a chance to find out what it's all about.'

'The gunman's a young punk named Alberto Thomaso,' the inspector growled. 'He's kidnaped a woman and was making the ransom call when we traced it to this tavern. You think maybe he's got his kidnap victim up there too?'

'I couldn't say, sir.' Turning to a nearby policeman who stood with a drawn revolver in his hand, the lieutenant said,

'Come over here, Thompkins.'

Obediently, the cop came over. He was a round-faced, middle-aged cop with the beginnings of a paunch.

'Was anybody with this guy when you jumped him?' the lieutenant asked.

'No, sir. He was all alone and just coming out of the tavern. We pulled up to the curb, jumped out of the car, and were just closing in on him when he pulled a gun and plugged Healey through the shoulder. By the time I got my gun out, he'd run back into the tavern. I guess he intended to go out the place's back door, but there's three doors back there and he got the wrong one. One leads out to the alley, one downstairs to the restrooms, and one to the flat upstairs. He picked the last door, and by then I was in the tavern and he didn't have time to change his mind. When I threw a shot at him, he ran up the stairs.'

'You sure he's still up there?' Day asked.

'There's nowhere else he could go. The tavern keeper told me he lives in the flat, and that stairway is the only entrance.

The tavern keeper had a gun under the bar, so I set him to watching the stair door, shooed all the customers out, and made a quick call for help over the car radio. Then, until help arrived, I covered the areaway between the two buildings to make sure he didn't try to slip across.'

I asked, 'Anybody but Alberto up there?'

Thompkins shook his head. 'The tavern keeper says no. He lives alone.'

Mouldy Greene said in a calm voice, 'Well, what we waiting for, Sarge? Let's go in and get this punk.'

22

Warren Day gave Mouldy an irritated look. 'Listen, Greene, you're just an innocent bystander here. What makes you think you're going anywhere?'

Mouldy looked astonished. 'Isn't this the guy who snatched Fausta?'

'Let's let the cops run things, Mouldy,' I suggested kindly. 'This sort of thing is their business.'

Mouldy's expression turned dubious, but since he had never quite gotten over the army habit of regarding me as his sergeant, he subsided temporarily in order to await developments.

Day turned to Patrolman Thompkins. 'You're certain he didn't slip across to the next building while you were making your last radio report?'

'He couldn't have,' the patrolman said positively. 'The guy who owns the tavern says there's no trap onto the roof. And the only two windows on the areaway side aren't anywhere near the windows in the next building. He might have reached the roof if he was athletic enough — by climbing out a rear window and pulling himself up over the edge of the parapet — but he couldn't have done it in the time it took me to get the areaway covered. Besides, it would take a Tarzan to make the roof that way, and from what I saw of this guy, he was no Tarzan.'

'Maybe he went down instead of up,' the inspector suggested.

This time the lieutenant answered. 'No, sir. I checked both the back of the building and the side Thompkins couldn't see. It's a thirty-foot drop from the windows on both sides, and there's nothing to climb down. The back is a brick courtyard, and the side a concrete sidewalk. If he'd jumped, he'd be lying on the ground with a couple of broken legs.'

The inspector scowled across at the windows again. 'The same things that make it tough for him to get out make it tough for us to get in. And I want this lad taken alive. He's an important witness in a homicide case, and also we don't know where he's concealed the woman he's kidnaped. How do you plan getting him out of there, Lieutenant?'

'I've sent for a scaling ladder. I thought I'd get some men on the roof next door and have them put a few tear-gas shells through the windows. That should bring him back down the stairway. Meantime, I thought I'd take a crack at talking him down as soon as things out here were organized.'

Things had pretty well organized themselves while we talked to the lieutenant. Ropes were now tautly stretched across the street and across two sides of the corner intersection, and police had managed to get all the curious onlookers beyond the ropes. Men with riot guns kept a steady watch on the dark windows of the flat.

After glancing around, the lieutenant said, 'I guess everything's under control. I'm going inside.'

And, casually, he stepped out into the glare of the spotlights and started across the street. Clamping down on his unlighted cigar, Day immediately followed.

I hesitated for a moment. Then, hoping

that Alberto was occupied at the moment in peering out either the side or back windows instead of the front, I started across briskly.

I kept my eyes fixed on the upper windows, noting both were raised a few inches from the bottom, and expecting to see a gun barrel protrude from one or the other at any instant. It could hardly have taken more than thirty seconds to cross the street, but the time seemed to drag interminably.

I was halfway across before I realized Mouldy Greene was right by my side. I realized it when he suddenly asked, 'What's there to whistle about?'

As a kid, I had lived for a time in a neighborhood near a cemetery, and I recall that whenever I had to traverse that particular block at night, I always whistled 'Yankee Doodle.' Now, with something of a shock, I realized I was whistling 'Yankee Doodle' through my teeth.

Cutting it off in the middle of a bar, I snarled at Mouldy with unnecessary savagery: 'I'm whistling past the grave-yard.'

Either Alberto wasn't at the front windows when we crossed, or I had overestimated his probable resentment at my fingering him, because no shot came from above. I breathed a sigh of relief as we passed through the tavern's front door.

Inside, I discovered the tavern consisted of a single long room with a bar running lengthwise from one end to the other. An electric grill at the far end seemed to be all the kitchen the place possessed. Near the front door was the phone booth from which Alberto had presumably called. The rear wall contained three doors. Over one a sign read 'Restrooms.' The second, I assumed was the rear exit, for the third door was open and I could see a stairway going upward as far as the first landing. That was as far as the stairs could be seen, because at the landing they made a ninety-degree left turn.

With both elbows on the bar to steady himself, a uniformed cop covered the stairway with a riot gun. Another cop, a pistol in his hand, waited to one side of the stairway door. In the far corner, well out of the probable line of fire, a middle-aged man who was apparently the tavern owner sat at a table, nervously sipping at a beer.

'Any sound from up there?' the lieutenant asked the cop with the riot gun.

Without removing his eyes from the stairway, the policeman said, 'Not a peep, sir. You sure he's up there?'

'He has to be. There isn't anywhere he could have gone.'

He started toward the stairs, but I stopped him by calling, 'Lieutenant.'

When he turned to look at me, I said, 'I've had a couple of dealings with this boy, Lieutenant. I also know more about the background of this situation than you do. I think if I talked to him, I might be able to advance some arguments for giving himself up that you wouldn't know about.'

He eyed me for a moment, then glanced questioningly at Warren Day. The inspector looked me over moodily.

Finally Day said, 'If you just want to

talk, Moon. From the foot of the stairs. I don't want you going up there and getting shot.'

'I'm not anxious to get shot,' I told him.

Since my experience of walking into my flat and being confronted by Alberto's gun, I had been carrying my P-38. Now I drew it, clicked off the safety, and approached the foot of the stairs.

'Listen, Al,' I called. 'The place is surrounded and you haven't got a chance. But we're more interested in the guy who hired you than we are in you, Al. Give yourself up and turn state's evidence, and the cops will give you every break possible. We want Walter Ford's killer more than we want you.'

When there was still no sound, I called in a louder tone, 'If you're willing to put the finger on Ford's killer, I'll even talk Fausta into dropping the kidnap charge, providing you haven't harmed her. So far, all you've done is winged a cop. Shoot it out and you're either going to get killed, or kill somebody and end up in the gas chamber. Give up and I'll guarantee to do everything possible to get you a light sentence.'

All the answer I got was more silence.

A little impatiently, I yelled, 'How about it, Al?'

The answer came suddenly and unexpectedly. Apparently he leaped like a cat from the top step to the landing, for one instant the landing was vacant, and the next instant he was crouched there as though he had materialized out of thin air, the twin of the Colt Woodsman I had taken from him gripped in his hand and centering on my head.

My own gun was drooping downward at a forty-five-degree angle, and there was no time to bring it up. There was no time to do anything but drop flat on my face.

His small-caliber gun popped just as I started to drop, and the shot was so close I could feel the heat of the slug on the top of my head as it whispered by. As I rolled to one side of the doorway, it popped twice more, gouging splinters from the wooden floor where I had sprawled a microsecond before.

Then the riot gun roared.

It was all over when I climbed shakily to my feet. The young gunman had taken the full blast of the riot gun square in the chest. He was dead before he started to tumble down the stairs.

'I wanted that man alive!' Warren Day screeched at the man who had fired.

The cop looked abashed. 'He was shooting, sir,' he said timidly.

'He had legs!' Day yelled at him, his long nose nearly dead white. 'Couldn't you shoot his legs?'

'Oh, stop your yelling,' I said, irked at him. 'The only way you could have taken him alive was to have me dead. He didn't want to be alive. He wanted to go down shooting, like a two-bit hero. The officer here just did what he had to.'

Day swung his thin nose at me. 'When I want your advice on what to say to my subordinates, I'll ask for it, Moon!'

'If you don't want it, don't practice your Simon Legree personnel policy in front of me then,' I snarled back at him. 'Pull it in private.'

We stood glaring at each other, both of us juvenilely taking out our rage at the loss of our star witness on the other, until Mouldy Greene brought us back to earth.

Mouldy asked of no one in particular, 'Now how the hell we going to ask him where he hid Fausta?'

23

Mouldy's question made us realize we had more important things to do than snarl at each other. With a grunt which I interpreted to mean he was willing to drop the argument, the inspector turned away.

In the hope that we might find some clue to Fausta's whereabouts in the dead man's pockets, Day and I searched the body. But the search told us nothing. A cheap new wallet of the type you can buy in dime stores — presumably purchased by Alberto as a temporary replacement for the wallet he had left behind when he tumbled backward out of the cottage window — contained only a few bills, and no papers whatever. Aside from the usual trivia you might find in any man's pockets, such as change, cigarettes, matches and a handkerchief, we found only two items of even faint interest. One was a small but vicious-looking leather sap filled with sand, and the other a tarnished brass key to a Yale lock.

'This might be the key to wherever he hid Miss Moreni,' the inspector said. 'He must have her locked up someplace, and this is the only key on him.'

'Fine,' I said. 'All we have to do is try every door in the city. Including the inside doors, since there's no label on it saying it isn't just a room key.'

'You don't think very fast, Moon,' the inspector said sourly. He handed the key to the uniformed lieutenant. 'Get a house-to-house canvass started, with this place as an axis. You're looking for a good-looking blonde of about twenty-seven.' He turned his eyes to me. 'Know how she was dressed, Moon?'

'Probably in an evening gown,' I said. 'We were supposed to go out tonight.'

Mouldy Greene said, 'She had on a green formal held up by her neck.'

When we both looked at him, he elaborated, 'Just by a kind of cloth dog collar, I mean. No shoulder straps.'

Warren Day turned back to the lieutenant. 'That ought to be enough of a description to make her stand out in this neighborhood. My hunch is, she's somewhere nearby, as I don't imagine Alberto would want to go too far for a phone; and he wouldn't want to leave her alone too long, even if he's got her tied up. You've got Thomaso's description, you've got the girl's, and you've got a key. I'll give you two hours to find her.'

'Yes, sir,' the lieutenant said, saluted, and left the tavern.

There was nothing more we could do but await the results of the canvass. I went back to El Patio with Mouldy to wait, and the inspector went home. Before he left, Day had calmed down enough to be a little ashamed of his previous display of temper, and he made oblique amends by brusquely instructing one of the remaining cops to phone me at El Patio the moment there was any news of Fausta.

The lieutenant managed to make the deadline Warren Day had set, but he only just made it. It took the police almost exactly two hours to locate Fausta. By then it was after one a.m., El Patio was closed, and Mouldy and I were seated at the bar alone when the call came.

It was from the cop Day had instructed to phone me, and all he could tell me was that Fausta had been found tied and gagged in a rooming house, she was unharmed, and she was at that moment on her way to El Patio in a squad car.

'You'll have to get the details from Miss Moreni,' he said. 'I wasn't with the team that found her, and all I know is what the lieutenant told me.'

Fifteen minutes later, Fausta came in, escorted by two large policemen. Ordinarily, Fausta is immaculate, but now her green formal was wrinkled, her lipstick smeared all over her face from the gag that had been in her mouth, and her blonde hair was tumbled every which way.

I am not very demonstrative, particularly before an audience, but after the strain of the last few hours my first impulse was to grab Fausta in my arms and kiss her. I got as far as rising from my bar stool before I noticed the expression in her eyes, then hurriedly changed my mind and reseated myself.

Fausta stopped directly before me, balled fists on her hips, and her lovely brown eyes flashed fire.

'Manny Moon, this is all your fault!' she announced. 'If you would get yourself a decent job instead of working at this horrible profession that gets you mixed up with . . . '

Then she caught sight of herself in the bar mirror and stopped short, an expression of horror growing on her face. Turning her back on all of us, she ran toward the powder room.

When Fausta finally rejoined us, she was as immaculate as usual except for the wrinkles in her gown. Apparently she had calmed somewhat, but there was still a dangerous glitter in her eyes.

'Just what has been going on tonight, my one?' she demanded of me.

'I thought you'd be able to tell me,' I said mildly.

'I was talking to you on the phone when this man came out of the closet,' she said. 'He hit me with something, and the next thing I knew I was lying on a bed in a damp basement, tied up and gagged.

Why do you allow such men in your apartment? And what are you going to do about catching him?'

'He's been caught, Fausta. He's dead.'

Her eyes grew wide. 'You . . . you killed him, Manny?' she asked weakly.

'A cop killed him,' I said. 'He tried to outshoot the cop's riot gun with a twenty-two pistol. Don't feel bad about it. He's no great loss.'

'Who was he?' she whispered.

'A young hood named Alberto Thomaso. Somebody hired him to kidnap you. We think his boss must have been Walter Ford's killer, but we aren't sure because Alberto died without talking. Did he tell you anything at all?'

Fausta shook her head. 'I did not even see him, except for a flashing glimpse from the corner of my eye just before he hit me. When I woke up, I was tied and he was gone.'

Patrolman Larkins put in, 'The lieutenant who detailed us to bring Miss Moreni home said they found her in a basement room over on Third, about four blocks from some tavern. I didn't understand

243

what tavern he was talking about.'

'The one the kidnaper phoned from,' I said.

Fausta said, 'That must be the lieutenant who was talking to the landlady where they found me. I heard her tell him the man who kidnaped me rented the room only that morning. The lieutenant said he guessed he picked it because it had a private entrance to the alley and he could come and go without being seen. They found a stolen panel truck in the alley, and they think he used that to take me from your apartment.'

I asked Fausta if she didn't think we ought to have a doctor look at her to make sure she didn't have a concussion from Alberto's leather sap.

'I am all right except for a little headache,' she said. 'See the bump I have?'

Turning her back to me, she lifted the blonde tresses over one ear to disclose a small black-and-blue lump.

'I'm sorry,' I said.

'Is that all?'

'I'm very sorry.'

'Fix it up,' she said imperiously.

Fausta knows I regard such antics as kissing a hurt to make it well as puerile, which was why she demanded the attention. She was merely taking her small revenge for being involved in what, to understate the matter, had been an unpleasant evening.

I looked at Mouldy, who only grinned at me. The two cops looked politely disinterested.

Rather self-consciously, I leaned forward and lightly kissed the bruise.

That was a mistake, for I might have known she wouldn't let it drop there.

'That is better,' she said briskly, dropping her hair back in place and turning to face me. 'But the gag also bruised my lips.'

She looked at me expectantly, and I growled, 'I'll fix that later.'

'Go ahead, Sarge,' Mouldy advised. 'Don't let us bother you.'

'Go to hell,' I said.

'Manny is bashful,' Fausta informed the two cops in a conspiratorial aside. 'Would one of you like to fix my hurt?'

'Manny is also jealous,' I announced. 'The first Swede or Irishman who takes that invitation will have to gum his food in the future.'

Then, since she was asking for it, I grabbed Fausta's wrist, jerked her up against me and kissed her right in front of Mouldy and the two cops.

The minute our lips touched, I not only lost my inhibitions, I lost my awareness that we had an audience. But, just before smoke began to issue from my ears, I was reminded that we did have one.

Mouldy Greene burst into wild applause.

Pushing Fausta away, I said to Mouldy, 'You're a moron,' and walked behind the bar to mix myself a drink.

'Fix a couple of nightcaps for the officers while you are back there,' Fausta said in a deliberately smug voice.

She knows it infuriates me when she turns smug after succeeding in making me drop my reserve.

24

On the assumption that since the killer had become panicky enough to have Fausta kidnaped once, he might try it again, I laid down some rules before I left El Patio.

'I don't want you to leave the club alone for anything,' I instructed Fausta. 'If you have to go out, take Mouldy with you.'

'All right, Manny,' Fausta said agreeably.

The next morning I got up at the unearthly hour of nine for the second day in a row. By ten, I was calling at Ed Friday's office.

The office was in the Russo Building, and while it was furnished expensively enough in a quiet sort of way, there was nothing about it to indicate it was supreme headquarters for several legitimate corporations plus a number of extralegal activities. The gold lettering on the frosted-glass door merely read, 'Friday Enterprises, Inc.' and inside there were only two rooms.

The outer room was quite large, probably sixty by thirty feet, and was divided into two sections by a polished brass railing which had a swinging gate in its center. The larger section contained a bank of filing cabinets and a dozen desks behind which clerks and stenographers were working.

The smaller section, just inside the door, contained a number of comfortable easy chairs, a sofa, several smoking stands, a table of magazines, and a red-haired receptionist behind a small desk.

It also contained Ed Friday's oversized bodyguard, Max Furtell, who lounged at ease reading a magazine.

The redhead started to ask me what she could do for me, but Max broke in, 'I'll take it, Ann.'

Ignoring him, I said to the girl, 'Mr. Friday in?'

Max came erect lazily, grinned at me without humor, and moved through the swinging gate toward a frosted-glass door marked 'Private.'

Three or four minutes passed before Max again appeared in the doorway of the room marked 'Private.' He was still grinning in a humorless sort of way when he crooked his finger at me. He managed to make the gesture deliberately condescending.

From behind the desk, Ed Friday's rubbery voice said, 'Good morning, Mr. Moon. I'm a little busy today, but I can give you ten minutes.'

Pulling one of the guest chairs away from the wall, I put it alongside his desk — facing the edge of the table, so that when I sat down I could see both Friday and Max. For some reason, I didn't feel like having the bodyguard behind me.

Friday said, 'I suppose you're here about Walter Ford again.'

'Partly,' I said. 'Also about Daniel Cumberland and Fausta Moreni.'

Friday looked blank.

'Cumberland was Ford's partner in a blackmail racket,' I explained. 'Seems he was murdered within a matter of hours of when Ford got it. And Miss Moreni was kidnaped last night in a rather stupid attempt to get me to drop the investigation.'

'Kidnaped? Is she still missing?'

I shook my head. 'The kidnaper didn't know calls could be traced to pay phones, and the cops met him as he walked out of a booth. Young punk named Alberto Thomaso. Says he works for you.'

For a moment, Friday looked at me without expression. Then he lifted a newspaper from his desk, thumbed through it until he found the item he wanted, and began to read in a toneless voice:

''A young gunman identified as Alberto Thomaso, 21, of 1812 Sixth Street, was killed in a gunfight with police at Swert's Tavern, Fifth Street and Martin, shortly after eleven p.m. last night, the police reported today. Approached for questioning as he left the tavern by radio-car patrolmen Thomas Healey and George Thompkins, Thomaso drew a gun and fired, inflicting a minor shoulder wound on Healey. He then fled back into the tavern, and was driven upstairs into a flat above the business by fire from Patrolman

Thompkins. The latter summoned assistance by means of his car two-way radio, and police quickly surrounded the building. In attempting to shoot his way out of the trap, Thomaso was killed by Patrolman Donald Murther.''

Friday looked up at me calmly. 'It doesn't mention Miss Moreni. Further on the item says the reason the cops were looking for Thomaso was to question him about an attempted kidnaping. But it goes on to say he died before he could be questioned. I always read the paper first thing in the morning, Mr. Moon.'

I conceded the first round. 'Let me put it this way then. Thomaso didn't live long enough to say he worked for anyone, but all indications point to you as his boss.'

I used my fingers to tick off points. 'First, it keeps recurring to me that you tried to get me to leave town the minute you suspected I might begin looking into the Ford case. Second, the motive behind Fausta's kidnaping was exactly the same thing: to force me to leave town. Third, of all the people involved in this case, you're the only one likely to have underworld connections with a hood like Thomaso. Any comments?'

'Yes,' Friday said in his rubbery voice. 'I've been pretty patient with you up to now, Moon. But now that you're actually accusing me of engineering two murders and a kidnaping, my patience is exhausted.' He looked at his bodyguard. 'Max, throw him out. And this time, I mean physically.'

For an instant the big man looked puzzled, but then he apparently decided if I wanted to make it easy for him, he wouldn't look a gift horse in the mouth. Moving forward, he snaked both enormous hands toward my shoulders.

I smashed the sole of my left foot against his right knee.

The blow should have cracked his kneecap, but apparently the man was strung together with piano wire instead of ordinary muscle. Instead of his knee buckling backward, his foot just flew out from under him.

As he started to fall forward, I let him have an elbow across the forehead. His head jolted back and his hands plunked down on the wooden arms of my chair to support himself. Bringing up my aluminum foot, I planted it in his stomach and pushed.

This was a mistake, because Max had a weight advantage of approximately sixty pounds. Instead of hurling him across the room as I intended the kick to, it merely straightened him up so that he could regain his balance. But it tipped my chair over backward.

I did a complete back somersault and bounced to my feet with my back in the corner of the room farthest from the door. Seeing that he had me treed, Max took his time about renewing the attack. First he shook his right leg tentatively to determine if it still worked. Apparently it did, though it must have been sprained from the terrific kick I had landed on his kneecap.

Deciding it would support him, he limped toward me with a snarl on his face.

I ducked a whistling right, slipped under his arm, and planted a solid left hook on his jaw as he swung around to face me again. He didn't even change expression.

The next thirty seconds were a

nightmare. I hit him six times with blows that would have put most pro fighters down for the count, but the only damage I could detect was to my knuckles. During the same time I managed to avoid four of his swings, any one of which would have knocked me through a wall if they had connected. Three times I ducked under his swinging arm and changed sides, catching him with solid hooks as he spun to face me again.

I had the advantage of speed and a professional knowledge of boxing, but it was only a question of time before one of his powerhouses connected and ended the fight. Fortunately, Max picked a time when my back was to the corner to change his tactics.

Tiring of swinging at a moving target, he suddenly lowered his head and charged. I skipped aside, added impetus to his charge by grabbing his shoulder and heaving as he went by, and he crashed head-on into the wall.

He knocked himself out.

As violent as the action had been for a few moments, it had been a relatively silent fight. Our feet shuffling on the carpet had made little sound, and the only noise aside from our panting had been the splat of my knuckles against his jaw and the crack of Max's head against the wall. Apparently no one in the outer office heard anything, for no one came to investigate, and the continued clatter of typewriters from the outer room indicated work was going on as usual.

Ed Friday had sat quietly behind his desk watching while the fracas went on. Now he looked from his recumbent bodyguard to me, glanced thoughtfully at the door, then looked back at me again as though he realized he couldn't expect much help from an office full of women. From his expression, you couldn't have told that he was in the last disturbed.

I rolled Max over on his back, felt his pulse and thumbed back an eyelid.

'That should have fractured his skull, but he's only knocked out,' I decided. 'He must have a steel plate in his head.'

Friday asked in a calm voice, 'You plan a little violence on me now, Mr. Moon?'

'It's your choice,' I told him. 'We're

going to have a talk. If you like, I'll slap you around until you feel conversational, but I'd prefer to skip further exercise.'

He let a slight smile form on his lips. 'Sit down, Mr. Moon.'

Righting my chair, I resumed my seat and lit a cigar. 'Let's start with why you wanted me to go to Mexico.'

Thoughtfully, he contemplated his bodyguard's horizontal figure. Finally he said, 'I'm going to be frank with you, Mr. Moon. Not because I'm afraid of getting slapped around, as you put it, but because my concern in this matter isn't worth getting involved in a possible murder rap. I want you to understand I had nothing to do with Ford's death and don't know who killed him. But I do have a reason for not wanting anyone to delve too closely into Ford's background. I was afraid you might turn up something that would louse up a business deal I have cooking. I'm not going to tell you what that deal is, because it's still cooking. But if it comes to the point where the police actually accuse me of having Ford killed, I'll sacrifice the deal in order to clear myself.

That will lose me some money, and it still won't solve your murder. I think you can understand why I don't want to talk about it unless it becomes necessary to clear myself.'

I thought this over for a few moments. 'I'm not a blabbermouth,' I said eventually. 'Suppose you get me off your neck by explaining the deal, with the understanding that I keep it confidential?'

He shook his head. 'You couldn't keep it confidential. After our conversation at your place the other night, I had you thoroughly investigated, and my report is that you have an almost unreasonably rigid code of ethics. If I'd known it at the time, I never would have attempted to bribe you. However, I know it now, and I'm certain if I told you about my business deal, you'd feel morally obligated to report it to the police.'

'You mean the deal is illegal?'

'Not on my part. I suspect one of the other parties to the arrangement has done something illegal though, and if it ever came to light, my part of it would blow up too. I haven't any actual knowledge of my associate's illegal act. It's only a suspicion, and you can't be held liable as an accessory for concealing a mere suspicion. I myself haven't done a thing I could be charged with, and I don't have your moral compulsion to report suspected illegal acts of others to the police. Particularly when it would cost me money.'

When I merely sat looking at him for a time without speaking, he went on, 'Your theory that no one but me would be able to contact a professional criminal like Thomaso is hogwash anyway. Anybody can contact any type of criminal he wants to hire simply by making the rounds of the slum taverns, keeping his ears open, and dropping a few discreet hints when he runs into a likely prospect. If this Thomaso kid was a freelance and in the habit of hanging around the rattier bars, anybody might have hired him.'

Max, seemingly intent on disproving my estimate of how long he would be out, groaned again and sat up at that moment. He was still groggy, however, and he kept his eyes closed while he pressed both hands to the top of his head.

With his powers of recuperation, he would probably be on his feet and raring to resume activities within another minute or so, I thought. And, since it looked as though I had obtained as much information from Ed Friday as I was likely to get unless I planned to tie him up and hold burning cigarettes against his feet, I decided to take my departure while Max was still in a daze.

Rising, I said to Friday, 'Thanks for nothing. You've been damn little help,' and walked out just as Max began to open his eyes.

25

But actually what Ed Friday had told me had been of some help. Not much, but at least it gave me the glimmer of a new idea.

While it was possible that everything he had said was pulled out of thin air in order to stall me off until his bodyguard rejoined the conversation, it was equally possible that he had been telling the truth. I inclined to take a middle course and accept his story as embroidered truth.

Never having been quite happy about Friday as the engineer of Ford's murder, I was inclined to believe his explanation that his attempt to steer me away from the case stemmed from concern that I might uncover something in Ford's background which would upset one of Friday's business deals. But I was equally inclined to doubt that the illegal act Friday mentioned was merely suspected by him. I believed that whatever the illegal act of his 'associate' had been, Friday did not merely suspect it, but had proof of it.

It seemed unlikely to me he would have gone as high as two thousand dollars to get me to refuse Ford's case if he had only a vague suspicion that his business deal was in danger.

What particular deal he had been talking about, it was of course impossible to say, as his interests were so varied; it could be anything from stock-market shenanigans to a corporation merger. However, it was just possible Friday's 'business deal' was his backing of the Huntsafe Company. The possibility made it at least worth looking into.

Stopping at a drugstore, I phoned Madeline Strong.

'You just caught me going out the door,' she said. 'I was on my way over to the jail to see Tom. Anything new?'

'Nothing concrete. I just developed the beginning of a wild new theory. Tell me, Madeline, where did your brother Lloyd live just before he died?'

'With me. We always lived together.'

'At the apartment you live in now?'

'Oh, no,' she said. 'In our old family

home over on Euclid. We were both born there, and after the folks died we just continued to live there. After Lloyd was killed, the place was too big for just me alone, so I moved here.'

'And sold the house, I suppose.'

'Well, it's for sale, but there haven't been any takers. It's too big for what most people want nowadays.'

'Lloyd's stuff still there? His papers and records, I mean?'

'Everything's there. Except dishes and a few pieces of furniture I moved here. I've been meaning to have a household sale one of these days, but just haven't gotten around to it.'

'Forget your visit to the jail,' I said. 'I want you to meet me at the house. What's the address?'

'1421 Euclid.'

'Suppose we meet there in twenty minutes?'

'All right,' Madeline said.

'Don't forget the key,' I advised, and hung up.

When I arrived at 1421 Euclid, I understood why the place had been unable to find a taker. It was an attractive enough white frame building in apparently good condition and with a wide, tree-shaded lawn on all four sides. But it was big enough to serve as a hospital. From the outside I judged it contained at least twenty rooms.

On the front lawn there was a slim metal post supporting a horizontal bar from which hung a gold-lettered sign. The sign read, 'C. Maurice Strong,' and the moment I saw it I suddenly realized where all Madeline's money had come from, and why she had seemed so surprised that I didn't know who she was the day I had asked her if she could afford my fee.

In the field of electronic invention, C. Maurice Strong was about second in line to Thomas Edison. Both he and his wife had died in an auto accident about four years before, I recalled, and I remembered that in the feature articles appearing in all the local papers after his death, the list of his inventions had been longer than his obituary. Just to mention a couple of random items, he had owned about half the patents in the fields of radio and television, and once had received a citation from the government for turning over to it without charge his patents on radar and automatic gun control.

I had been waiting for about five minutes when Madeline arrived in a taxi.

'Why didn't you tell me your father was C. Maurice Strong?' I asked as we walked toward the broad front porch.

She looked at me in surprise. 'Didn't you know?'

'How would I know?' I asked reasonably. 'Strong's a fairly common name.'

'I guess I just take it for granted everybody knows.'

Inside, the house was pervaded by the unused, dusty smell of having been locked up a long time. White dustcovers were over all of the furniture.

Madeline led the way through a huge front room, a slightly smaller dining room, and into a wide back hall. She opened a door leading off the hallway and preceded me down a flight of stairs to the basement.

'Lloyd's laboratory is down here in the basement,' Madeline explained. 'He kept all his records in the lab.'

We had to pass through a games room

and a laundry room before we reached the laboratory, which was under the front part of the house. It was a large room, about twenty by fifteen feet, with an electrical workbench — similar to the one I had seen in Barney Amhurst's apartment — along one wall.

'He kept everything in there,' Madeline said, pointing to a single dusty filing cabinet in one corner. 'What is it you're looking for?'

'I'm not sure,' I said. 'I'll just have to go through everything.'

Madeline drew a chair away from the workbench, looked at the dust on it, and decided to continue standing. 'It's already been gone through once, you know. After the funeral we had to check through his papers for the will, insurance policies, and so on.'

'Who's we?' I asked.

'Well: me, I mean, actually. But Walter Ford helped me.'

I had just pulled open the top drawer of the filing cabinet, but instead of looking down into it, I looked over my shoulder at Madeline.

'What was that?' I asked

'I said, Walter Ford helped me go through the papers.'

I frowned at her. 'How did that happen? I thought you only knew Ford casually before he came into the Huntsafe Company.'

'I did,' Madeline said. 'Well, it was a little more than casually. He'd had some business relationships with my father and was a great admirer of his. Lloyd and I had known him for years, but he was older than we were, so we never went around in the same crowd. I think he came to Lloyd's funeral more because of admiration for my father than because Lloyd meant anything to him. But he was very considerate. You know how people at a funeral always ask if there is anything they can do?'

I nodded in indication that I knew.

'Well, my lawyer had told me I would have to go through all Lloyd's papers, and I was thinking about it and dreading the task when Walter came up and asked if there was anything he could do. So I said, yes, he could help me sort through Lloyd's papers.'

I raised an eyebrow. 'Why him particularly? Don't you have any close relatives?'

She shook her head. 'None that live here. And because of Walter's feelings for my father, I kind of felt that he was like an uncle or something. I don't mean all the time. But during the emotional stress of the funeral. About the only other person I could have asked was Barney, and he was so broken up over Lloyd's death I couldn't ask him.'

'I see. And I suppose Ford did most of the sorting?'

'Well, yes. I'm not very good at that sort of thing.'

Since Walter Ford had been at the file before me, there was little chance I would find what I was looking for, I realized. With his propensity for blackmail, it would have gone into his inside pocket the moment he found it. Nevertheless, I doggedly went through every drawer of the cabinet.

In a manila folder marked 'Tax Returns,' I found duplicate copies of Lloyd Strong's Federal 1040 forms for the three years before he died. Since there were no forms for previous years, I assumed that prior to these, whatever income he had was included on his father's annual return.

Checking over the three 1040s, I found that most of the income reported was from royalties on patents inherited from his father, and from stock dividends and interests. The totals, I noted, came to quite impressive amounts. In each of the last two returns there was also included a Schedule C showing profit and loss on his own patents. For both years gross income amounted to less than two thousand dollars; and, after deducting business expenses, both years showed a substantial net loss.

The item which interested me most was line eleven of Schedule C, 'Salaries and wages not included in line four.'

For both years, Lloyd Strong claimed salary payments of $3,770.00.

I said to Madeline, 'Did you know your brother was losing money in the inventing business?'

'Oh, yes,' she said. 'But that was only temporary.'

'How do you mean?' I asked.

'It takes some time before royalties

begin to come in from patents. Lloyd had several excellent chances to sell some of his patents outright, but since we didn't need the money, he preferred to take a long-range view and only lease them on a royalty basis. It's only since Father died that Lloyd started patenting his inventions. And every patent he's leased is tied up with an ironclad contract. Returns are low to start with that way, but the eventual income should be four to five times what he could have gotten by outright sales. My brother was an excellent businessman.'

By then, it was pushing twelve-thirty, and I offered to buy Madeline lunch. We had it in an excellent restaurant she knew from having spent her whole life in the neighborhood. The food was fine, but the lunch was no fun, because Madeline kept pestering me to know what I had been looking for and I was in no mood to tell her.

'I want to talk to Warren Day before I say a word to anyone else,' I said. 'I think I've got the answer to this case, but there isn't a shred of proof. Before I lay myself open to a possible defamation of character suit, I want to see if Day can help me.'

'You mean you actually know who killed Walter Ford?'

'I've got a theory about it. It may come to nothing. And that's all you get until I find out.'

26

I found the inspector leaning back in his chair, hands clasped across his lean stomach, staring out the window with an unnatural expression on his face. After studying the expression for a moment, I came to the incredulous conclusion that it was geniality.

He cocked an eye at me and said affably, 'Hello, Manny.'

That unnerved me. When Day calls me 'Manny' instead of 'Moon,' he either wants a favor or has just received exceptionally good news.

'All this evidence of good cheer. If you're not careful, you'll get yourself expelled from the ogres' union.'

This brought a frown to his face, which made him look more normal. 'While I think of it, Moon, give me back that picture.'

I had forgotten I was still carrying around a piece of evidence. Taking the photograph of Bubbles and Daniel Cumberland from my pocket, I handed it to him. It disappeared into the top drawer of his desk.

'I'm going to cheer you up even more than you are, Inspector,' I said. 'This ought to make you delirious.'

'You're moving out of town,' he guessed.

I gave him a wounded look. 'Then who would do your work for you? No, but I've got a brand-new theory about the Ford-Cumberland case.'

'You're a little late,' he said. 'I've got more than a theory. I've got a solution.'

I raised my eyebrows.

'My idea of having the high schools run a check of their summer-school pupils paid off,' he said. I noted that it was now *his* idea instead of Hannegan's. 'We located the kid who had that gun initialed at Jessup's.'

'And found out who hired him?'

'Well, not yet. I just talked to the school principal over the phone. I sent Hannegan over to Fairmont High to pick the kid up. He ought to be back any minute now.'

In view of this development, I decided to keep my new theory to myself until we heard what the fake Pickup Service messenger had to say.

Eventually, there was a knock on the door, and Day yelled, 'In!'

The door opened and Lieutenant Hannegan ushered in a tall, thin youngster with a horse-like face. The boy seemed to be about sixteen or seventeen, and was dressed in denim slacks and a T-shirt.

'Eddie Johnson,' Hannegan said. 'Inspector Day. Moon.'

'Sit down, Eddie,' Day said in a friendly voice, pointing to a chair.

Gingerly, the youngster seated himself. He looked a little nervous, but not particularly scared.

'You're a student at Fairmont, are you?' the inspector asked in an obvious attempt to put the kid at ease.

'Yes, sir.' The 'yes' started in a bass voice, but the 'sir' came out soprano.

'You know why we want to talk to you, Eddie?'

'Yes, sir. Mr. Benson told me. He's our principal.'

'What did Mr. Benson tell you, Eddie?'

'Well, he asked over the loudspeaker if any of the students had run an errand to Jessup's Jewelry Store recently, and if they had, to report to the office. I reported, and Mr. Benson said the police were trying to locate the person I ran the errand for. But I don't think I'll be able to help you much, sir.'

Day frowned. 'Why not?'

'I don't know who she was.'

The statement brought both Day and me up straight in our chairs.

'Did you say *she*?' I asked.

'Yes, sir. It was a woman.'

The inspector said, 'We didn't expect you to know her name, Eddie. All we need is a description.' He gave me a pleased look. 'Seems our killer is a woman, Moon. That conform to your new theory?'

It knocked the props from under my new theory, but I didn't want to give Day the satisfaction of knowing that. I merely gave him an enigmatic smile.

'I don't know if I can describe her too good,' Eddie said dubiously. 'Except she was a nice-looking woman.'

'How did she contact you?'

'She just stopped me on the street after school and said she'd give me five bucks to run an errand for her. I said sure, and she took me in a taxi over to Jessup's. She gave me a big manila envelope with something heavy inside, and told me to tell the jeweler I was from Pickup Service.

'Well, I done like she said, and that's all there was to it. I give the envelope to the man in the store, walked out again, and got back in the taxi. The woman give me five bucks and dropped me off in front of the school, where she picked me up. Then, just before I got out, she told me to meet her the same place and the same time next day, and I could make another five bucks.

'So I did, and this time my job was to pick up the envelope and pay the charges on it. She give me a ten-dollar bill to pay for it with, and when I handed her back the change, she paid me off and had the taxi take me back to the school again. I never saw her since.'

'Okay, Eddie,' Day said. 'Now, to get back to this woman's description. Was she a blonde or a brunette?'

'I never saw her hair. She wore one of those scarf things around her head.'

The inspector frowned. 'About what age was she?'

'Not real old,' Eddie said vaguely. 'Around twenty or thirty. I'm not much good at guessing women's ages.'

'Just describe her as well as you can,' he said.

Eddie Johnson screwed his long face into a thoughtful frown. 'Well, she had a kind of pretty face and a nice shape. Not too fat and not too skinny. She wore just a plain dress. Blue, I think. And this light blue scarf around her head. I noticed she had nice legs.' He thought a moment and added, 'She was about average height.'

Day looked frustrated. 'That description fits half the women in town,' he said to me. 'I guess we'll just have to parade them all before him.'

'Parade half the women in town?' I asked.

'The ones connected with the case,' he said impatiently.

'And that's who?'

He gave me an irritated look. 'The women who were there the evening Ford got it. Evelyn Karnes, Bubbles Duval, Madeline Strong. Do I have to spell it out for you?' He paused a moment and added, 'Fausta Moreni.'

'Fausta had never even seen Walter Ford until an hour before he was dead,' I protested.

'We'll parade her anyway. I'm not playing any favorites. Hannegan, bring in the four women I just mentioned.'

As the lieutenant straightened away from the wall, I said, 'Hold it a minute. Are you planning to parade all four women at once and let Eddie pick one out?'

'That's the usual way,' Day said.

'Then you'll have to wait till tonight,' I told him. 'Unless you're mean enough to make Bubbles Duval lose her job by dragging her away from Saxon and Harder's in the middle of a fashion show. She works till seven.'

For a few moments he merely stared at me, his nose slightly whitening at the tip. Then he said, 'Oh, the hell with you, Moon.' At Hannegan he snarled, 'Arrange for all four women to be here at seven-thirty p.m. sharp.'

'One of them is in the building now,' I offered. 'Madeline Strong is back visiting Thomas Henry in his cell.'

The inspector grunted, picked up his desk phone, and instructed someone to bring Madeline Strong to his office.

Then he said to Eddie, 'I'm afraid you'll have to stay right here at headquarters until this is over, Eddie. We'll serve you some supper here. You can phone your folks and tell them where you are and that you're not in any trouble. You can use my phone, and if they're worried, I'll talk to them.'

There was a knock on the door.

'Just a minute,' Day called. To Hannegan he said, 'That's probably Miss Strong, and I don't want her to see Eddie or Eddie to see her until we can have a fair parade no shyster lawyer can break, with all four women present at the same time. Take him in the next room.'

As the lieutenant disappeared through the side door, the inspector called, 'Come in.'

It was Madeline Strong. 'You wanted to see me, Inspector?' she asked.

'Yes. Could you be down here at my office tonight at seven-thirty?'

'Tonight?' the girl asked. 'I'm supposed to be at Barney Amhurst's at eight.'

'Another party?' I asked dryly.

Apparently Madeline's session with her fiancé had gone well, for her voice was entirely friendly when she spoke. 'Not exactly, though I suppose Barney will serve drinks. It's more a business meeting to decide whether we should try to buy out Walter Ford's widow's share of Huntsafe. She inherits Walter's ten percent, you know.'

I had an idea. 'Then Friday will be there too?'

'Yes, of course.'

'And will he bring Evelyn Karnes?'

'I suppose. He usually does.'

To the inspector, I said, 'I've got a better idea than bringing everybody down here. Why disrupt so many people's plans? Let's have this meeting go ahead, and I'll get Fausta and Bubbles over to Barney's at eight too.'

The inspector threw up his hands.

'First you heckle me into postponing it till tonight, now you want it halfway across town. You run it any way you damn please, Moon.'

Rising, he stalked out of his office and slammed the door.

'What's the matter with him?' Madeline asked.

'Temperament,' I understated.

27

After Warren Day left us alone, I explained to Madeline that the inspector hoped to crack the case that evening, and it was essential none of the people who would be at Amhurst's know in advance anything was scheduled beyond the business meeting already arranged. I also asked her if, without arousing suspicion that anything unusual was underway, she could find out definitely whether or not Evelyn Karnes planned to be present.

Madeline said, 'That's easy,' and promptly used the inspector's phone to call Evelyn. On the feminine pretext that she wanted to know what Evelyn planned to wear, so that she could dress accordingly, she learned that Evelyn was going to Amhurst's with Ed Friday that evening.

I took it upon myself to get Bubbles and Fausta there.

When I phoned Fausta, she was a little difficult about arrangements, pretending to believe I had reached that stage of life where I felt I had to prove my romantic prowess by parading women in public.

'This isn't a date,' I explained patiently. 'Warren Day wants everyone present who was there the night of the murder. Would you rather I just pick Bubbles up and send Hannegan after you?'

Fausta sniffed. 'I will go with you since it is the inspector's wish. But you come for me first, Manny Moon.'

'Be ready at a quarter of eight,' I told her. 'And this isn't formal. A plain dress will do.'

Bubbles presented no such problem because I neglected telling her the circumstances. I merely phoned her shortly after seven, said I would be by to pick her up just before eight, and made no mention of the fact that I would have Fausta along.

As a matter of fact, I didn't let her find it out until I had escorted her from her door to the curb and held the car door open for her.

'What's this?' she asked then, staring at Fausta. 'You competing with King Farouk, Manny?'

'Get in,' I said. 'This isn't an evening of pleasure. We're going over to Barney Amhurst's to solve a couple of murders.'

Dubiously, Bubbles slipped into the seat next to Fausta.

It was shortly after eight when I pulled up in front of the Remley Apartments.

Apparently Ed Friday and Evelyn Karnes were already there, for the gray coupé of Friday's bodyguard stood in the same spot it had the night Ford was killed. I also spotted Warren Day's car parked across the street.

As I helped the two women out of my Plymouth, Max Furtell stepped from his coupé and limped over.

'Well, well,' he said to me. 'I kind of been hoping I'd run into you again.'

'I haven't time to play now, Max. Run along.'

Max grinned at me. 'Excuse me, ladies, but I've got a little unfinished business with your boyfriend.'

He was starting to reach out for a handful of shirtfront when Warren Day's voice said from behind him, 'Something on your mind, Furtell?'

'Oh, hello, Inspector,' Max said uneasily. 'I was just saying hello to Mr. Moon here.'

'So you've said it,' Day growled. 'Now climb back in your car and stay there.'

'Sure, Inspector.' He went back toward his car without looking at any of us.

As the inspector, the two women and I moved toward the apartment-house entrance, I asked Day, 'How about the kid?'

'He'll stay in the car with Hannegan until I make sure they're all here.'

Barney Amhurst seemed surprised to see us, but he acted the part of the perfect host. Inviting us in, he waved us all to chairs and asked what we would like to drink.

'Madeline and Friday and I have a little business to discuss,' he said. 'But it's nothing secret and it won't take long. We can have a party at the same time.'

'We didn't come for a party,' Warren Day said in a grim voice. 'I'm here on official business.'

He stared around at the assembly. Madeline Strong and the sleek Evelyn Karnes sat side by side on a sofa. Ed Friday had been seated in a chair by the fireplace, but rose when Fausta and Bubbles came in. When the two women found chairs, he seated himself again and nodded shortly to me.

'I guess everybody is here,' the inspector decided. 'Just stay put. I'll be back in a minute.'

As he disappeared again, Barney Amhurst stared, puzzled, at the door he had gone through. 'What's this all about, Moon?'

'The inspector won't be long,' I said. 'He'll explain when he comes back.'

Now that it seemed we were finally on the verge of breaking the case, I had been experiencing steadily mounting excitement. But when Day returned with Eddie Johnson and Hannegan in tow, there was an anti-climax. The boy stood in the center of the room, looked carefully from Fausta to Madeline to Bubbles to Evelyn, then slowly shook his head.

'None of these is the lady I ran the errands for,' he stated positively.

'What!' Day yelled, his nose instantly beginning to whiten.

'I can't help it,' Eddie said defensively.

'The right lady just isn't here.'

Day turned an accusing stare at me.

I said, 'Inspector, we've been working on the premise Ford was either shot, or hired shot, by someone who was here that night. It just occurred to me there's a fifth woman connected with the case. And she's got the best motive of all.'

When he only continued to stare at me, I said, 'Mrs. Jennifer Ford. She was having trouble collecting alimony from Walter, but as his widow she won't have a bit of trouble collecting his ten percent interest in the Huntsafe.'

'Hannegan,' the inspector snapped. 'Bring Mrs. Ford over here right away.'

'2212 Wright Street,' I offered helpfully. 'It's only about six blocks from here.'

When Hannegan had gone, I walked over to the door of Barney Amhurst's workroom, opened it. and felt alongside the door for the light switch.

'Want anything in particular?' Barney Amhurst asked from behind me.

My hand connected with the switch and I flicked it on. The place had been cleaned up, I noted. All the bloodstains had been removed, the broken glass swept up, and a fresh pane replaced the broken panel of the French door.

'Nothing in particular,' I said, preoccupied. 'Just refreshing my memory.'

Switching off the light again, I pulled the door shut.

To Warren Day I said, 'If it turns out Jennifer Ford is the woman who hired Eddie, that new theory I had still hangs together with a slight modification. Want to hear it?'

'What have I got to lose?' the inspector asked.

'What threw me off course was learning a woman had that gun initialed,' I said. 'Before that, I had it all figured out that a man was the killer. Now I think so again. I'm guessing the only part Mrs. Ford had in this was stealing a couple of her husband's pistols from his apartment, getting one initialed 'T.H.', and turning them both over to the killer.'

'You don't even know yet that she's the woman,' Day growled.

'I'm fairly certain of it now that I've got the cobwebs out of my brain,' I assured him. 'Everything fits all the way. Even Ed Friday's attempt to bribe me to leave town.'

'Leave me out of it,' Friday said in a ponderous voice.

'You let yourself in,' I told him. 'I doubt that we can make an accessory charge stick, but you know and I know that you've been aware of who Ford's killer was all along.'

The ex-racketeer emitted a snort. 'Why would I conceal a thing like that?'

'Because you knew the motive for the killing. You didn't care a hoot about either Ford or the killer, but you did care about your forty percent interest in the Hunt-safe. And you knew that the moment the motive came out, your agreement with Barney Amhurst wouldn't be worth the paper it was written on. Because Amhurst didn't have any legal right to make such an agreement.'

'Wait a minute,' Amhurst interrupted. 'What are you talking about?'

'About you,' I said. 'You've been trading off percentage interest in the Huntsafe left and right without owning a nickel's worth of what you were trading. The whole thing belongs to Madeline Strong.'

Madeline looked from Barney to me with a wondering expression on her face. 'What do you mean, Mr. Moon?'

I said, 'Let's start at the beginning, back with your brother's death. I've had three versions of that shooting. From Amhurst, Tom Henry and Bubbles. But I haven't heard yours. Want to tell it?'

She looked puzzled. 'What has Lloyd's death got to do with Walter's?'

'A lot, if my theory is correct. Tell me, after you discovered Lloyd was dead, what happened?'

'We walked into town and reported it. The state police went after the body.'

'All three of you walked into town?'

'No. Just Tom and I. Barney stayed with Lloyd's body.'

'I thought it would have been that way,' I said. 'That gave him plenty of time to remove something from it.'

When Amhurst opened his mouth to demand what I meant by that, I cut him off by saying, 'Amhurst claims he thought he heard another rifle crack at the same time you fired, Madeline. Do you recall any such thing?'

The girl shook her head slowly. 'There wasn't any other sound. I distinctly remember everything that happened. I don't think I'll ever forget. It was so quiet when I fired, I even recall I could hear Barney's watch ticking.'

I felt a little thrill run along my spine. 'His watch?' I asked. 'You're sure it was his watch?'

'Of course. What else?'

'The Huntsafe,' I said. 'You heard the ticking of the Huntsafe receiver strapped to Barney's wrist.'

The girl looked at me incredulously. Amhurst emitted a derisive snort.

'But the Huntsafe wasn't finished until a month ago,' Madeline said.

'It was finished back at the time of your hunting trip,' I corrected her. 'Amhurst just announced its perfection a month ago. He and your brother were giving it a field test under actual hunting conditions when Lloyd was killed. That's why Lloyd was in the line of fire. He deliberately got

290

himself where he wasn't supposed to be in order to demonstrate how the Hunt-safe could prevent accidental shootings. Only Barney, instead of avoiding shooting in that direction, deliberately used the gadget in order to locate Lloyd in the underbrush and kill him. With the needle pointing straight at Lloyd, Amhurst undoubtedly could spot where he was lurking and get an accurate bead on him.'

Barney Amhurst said, 'This is the worst nonsense I ever heard. Why, in heaven's name, would I want to kill my own partner?'

28

'Because he wasn't your partner,' I said. 'He was your employer. Only, nobody knew that but you and Lloyd. You killed him because it was the only way you could get control of the Huntsafe patent.'

Madeline was staring at Amhurst as though he were some kind of monster. 'I don't understand any of this,' she almost whispered.

'Then I'll explain it,' I told her. 'I got on the track when I got to thinking over the various facts I had gleaned about your brother's character. He was very close-mouthed about his affairs, for instance. Until after he was dead, no one but Barney Amhurst even knew he was working on the Huntsafe. Also, he was a sharp businessman. I recall your remarking he always had an ironclad contract for everything, and it was always in his favor. Ostensibly Lloyd and Barney were part-ners, but it occurred to me that Lloyd had a lot of inherited money, while Barney didn't. Lloyd could afford to experiment along, even for years, without income; but I wondered how Amhurst could. That got me to wondering if perhaps they weren't partners at all, but Lloyd had been paying Barney a salary as an assistant. Today, going through Lloyd's files, I learned he had been. His last two years' tax records showed he had been paying three thousand seven hundred and seventy dollars in salary a year. That works out to seventy-two dollars and fifty cents a week.'

Madeline said, 'He was paying that to Barney, and I didn't even know it?'

'You told me yourself he never discussed his business matters. Knowing Lloyd's character, I guessed that if he was paying Barney a salary, he would have an unbreakable contract with Barney giving himself full rights to anything developed through their joint efforts. I think it was that contract that got Ford killed. I think he found it when he was helping you sort over Lloyd's papers, realized it meant Amhurst had no legal right to the

Huntsafe at all, and used it to blackmail a ten percent interest from Amhurst.'

'Where is this so-called contract, then?' Amhurst demanded.

His voice was condescending, but I noticed sweat beading his upper lip.

I shrugged. 'Destroyed, probably. That's what you searched Daniel Cumberland's apartment for after you killed him. You must have gone there straight from taking Madeline home in a taxi that night. How you knew the contract was at Cumberland's instead of at Ford's place, I don't know, but it's a relatively unimportant point. Why'd you have to kill them both? Had they raised the ante beyond a ten percent interest, and made you realize they would bleed you white for the rest of your life?'

Warren Day broke in. 'Listen, Moon, are you accusing Amhurst himself of killing Ford and Cumberland? Or only of hiring young Thomaso to do it?'

'He only used Thomaso for odd chores,' I said. 'Amhurst did the actual killing.'

'How? By black magic? I'll swallow Cumberland, but how about Ford? He didn't have time to get the gun over to Henry's flat.'

'He didn't have to, Inspector. The whole thing was an optical illusion. Only an inventor would devise such an elaborate Rube Goldberg way to kill anyone. It would have been much simpler to have pushed Ford under a bus at some crowded intersection. Of course, this way he could frame Thomas Henry for the killing. And he wanted to do that because he's nuts about Madeline.'

'How did he do it?' Day shouted at me.

'Take it easy,' I said. 'I'm getting to it. The gun in Henry's workshop was planted *before* the crime. You'll recall it was identified as the murder weapon not by ballistic examination of the bullet, but by microscopic examination of the ejected casing. Apparently Amhurst knew a soft-nosed bullet almost certainly would be too battered to make comparison tests possible. So before he started out that evening, he must have laid the scene. I guess that this is what happened. He fired the gun initialed 'T.H.' somewhere — maybe at some isolated spot along the river. He saved the ejected casing to drop on the lawn outside his workroom window so that it would look as though the gun had been fired there. Then he let himself into Henry's flat by means of a skeleton key, planted the gun, and swiped one of Henry's pipes to drop near the shell.'

'How about the broken window?' Amhurst asked in a controlled voice. 'How did I fake that?'

'I'd guess it was broken in advance,' I told him. 'And the pieces carefully collected in an otherwise empty waste can. When you had us all gathered in here as witnesses, you took Ford into your workroom and left the door only an inch ajar so we could hear you but couldn't see you. Then, pretending to give Ford instructions, you started to say something in a loud voice about his taking one of the Huntsafes and coming back out here. At the same time you picked up the waste can, dumped the glass on the floor beneath the window so that it would sound as though it had just been broken from outside, then turned and shot Ford.'

'What did I do with the gun?' Amhurst

asked in the same controlled voice. 'I was searched, remember, and so was the workroom.'

'During the thirty seconds or so while I was getting up nerve enough to push open the door, you put it in the empty case of the Huntsafe transmitter you had in your hand.'

'It wasn't empty. I showed it to the inspector later.'

'That stumped me for a long time,' I admitted. 'But I think I've figured out how you did it. You had the works of the transmitter concealed in the bathroom. When you tore in there, supposedly to be sick, you simply took the gun out of the transmitter case and put the works back in. The murder gun was hidden in the bathroom all the time, but no one thought to search it.'

'When you said this was a Rube Goldberg plot, you hit it,' Amhurst said derisively. 'But the plot's all in your head.'

Even Warren Day was looking a little dubious about my theory. I brought forth some more arguments to clinch it.

'There isn't a single factor that doesn't

point straight at Amhurst, Inspector. For instance, when I made my first progress report over the phone to Miss Strong, Amhurst was at her apartment. As a matter of fact, he answered the phone. No one else knew I was making any progress, but that evening I found young Thomaso waiting at my apartment when I got home. Amhurst was also present when I reported to Madeline that I had learned it wasn't Walter Ford who had that gun initialed 'T.H.' That threw him into a blind panic, for that same evening he had Thomaso kidnap Fausta. Even the fact that Thomas Henry's phone was used to make those checkup calls points to Amhurst. We know the killer must have had a skeleton key to get into Henry's flat in order to plant the gun, and all Amhurst had to do was walk across two intervening lawns. I'll admit it's an incredible murder plot, but Amhurst here is a rather incredible guy. All through this thing he's shown a mixture of brilliant planning and impracticality. Both fit his character exactly. Especially the impracticality. He committed three murders to get his hands on an invention, then bargained away all but thirty percent interest in it because he hasn't an ounce of business sense. What more do you want?'

'Maybe he wants some proof,' Amhurst said.

Despite his controlled voice, now not only Amhurst's upper lip, but his forehead and even his cheeks, were covered with sweat. He began mopping at his face with a handkerchief.

Hannegan picked that moment to arrive with Mrs. Jennifer Ford. Mrs. Ford had apparently been at the gin again, for she was noticeably uncertain in her movements.

The moment she walked in, Eddie Johnson took one look at her and announced in a positive voice, 'That's the lady who hired me to run those errands, Inspector.'

Mrs. Ford turned pale. She stared at Eddie as though he were the ghost of her dead husband. Then she said, in a rapid but alcoholically thick voice, 'All I did was steal two of Walter's guns, have one of them initialed, and give them both to

Barney. I didn't have anything to do with Walter's death.'

'Why'd you steal the guns for him?' Warren Day barked at her.

'Barney said . . . Well, Walter wasn't paying me my alimony, and Barney said . . . '

When her voice trailed off to nothing, I finished for her. 'Barney said you could inherit a ten percent interest in the Huntsafe if you helped him, didn't he?'

She looked at me wide-eyed, and Barney Amhurst said in a low voice, 'You stupid alcoholic! If you'd kept your mouth shut, they couldn't have proved a thing. Now you've talked us both into the gas chamber!'

His face was now drenched with sweat, but he made no attempt to mop it dry.

The woman began to whimper.

We do hope that you have enjoyed reading this large print book.

Did you know that all of our titles are available for purchase?

We publish a wide range of high quality large print books including:
Romances, Mysteries, Classics
General Fiction
Non Fiction and Westerns

Special interest titles available in large print are:
The Little Oxford Dictionary
Music Book, Song Book
Hymn Book, Service Book

Also available from us courtesy of Oxford University Press:
Young Readers' Dictionary
(large print edition)
Young Readers' Thesaurus
(large print edition)

For further information or a free brochure, please contact us at:
Ulverscroft Large Print Books Ltd.,
The Green, Bradgate Road, Anstey,
Leicester, LE7 7FU, England.
Tel: (00 44) 0116 236 4325
Fax: (00 44) 0116 234 0205

TWEAK THE DEVIL'S NOSE

Richard Deming

Driving to the El Patio club to see his girlfriend Fausta Moreni, the establishment's proprietor, private investigator Manville Moon does not expect to be witness to a murder. As he steps from his car outside the club, he hears a gun suddenly roar from the bushes close behind him. Walter Lancaster, the lieutenant governor of the neighbouring state of Illinois, has been shot! The assassination will not only make headlines all over the country, but also place the lives of Moon and Fausta in deadly danger . . .

THE MAN WITH THE CAMERA EYES

Victor Rousseau

Investigative lawyer Langton has solved many bizarre cases with the help of his friend Peter Crewe, who possesses such an extraordinary photographic memory that he never forgets a face. Here Langton relates twelve stories featuring audacious jewel robberies, scientific geniuses gone mad and bad, and cold-blooded murder served up via amusement park rides, craftily concealed explosives, and hot air balloons. In each, the Man with the Camera Eyes provides the observations and deductions that are crucial to the solution of the mystery — often risking his own life in the process . . .

THE SEPIA SIREN KILLER

Richard A. Lupoff

Prior to World War II, black actors were restricted to minor roles in mainstream films — though there was a 'black' Hollywood that created films with all-black casts for exhibition to black audiences. When a cache of long-lost films is discovered by cinema researchers, the aged director Edward 'Speedy' MacReedy appears to reclaim his place in film history. But insurance investigator Hobart Lindsey and homicide officer Marvia Plum soon find themselves enmeshed in a frightening web of arson and murder with its roots deep in the tragic events of a past era . . .

KILLING COUSINS

Fletcher Flora

Suburban housewife Willie Hogan is selfish, bored, and beautiful, passing her time at the country club and having casual affairs. Her husband Howard doesn't seem to care particularly — until one night she comes home from a party to discover he has packed his things and intends to leave her for good. Panicked, Willie grabs Howard's gun and shoots him dead. With the help of her current paramour, Howard's clever cousin Quincy, the body is disposed of — but unbeknownst to either of them, their problems are only just beginning . . .